Illustrations and Photos:

Once More to the Rural: Teague von Bohlen

Aje: Erin & Erin

Animal Encounters, Ditch Driving: Maureen Hearty

Everything is a Cloud: Nina Elder

The Iowa School for the Blind: Charlie Fasano

The High Winds Blow: Ela Jones

Prairie Futures Colcha: Trent Segura

Cover photo of the Alma Motel in Joes, Colorado: One of Kirsten Stoltz's ancestors

Snoopy: Thomas Ray Hill

Various other images: Various other people

ISBN: 979-8-218-4-8865-9

Library of Congress ANT.FIC.SOC.0224.1974

The prose in this anthology is fiction except when it isn't. Places and people are not real unless they are.

the alma journal

A Prairie Sea Project

contents

Introduction vii
by Kirsten Stoltz, co-director of the Prairie Sea Project

ONCE MORE TO THE RURAL 1
A Week in Joes, Colorado
by Teague von Bohlen

THE OASIS 27
Seven Lives in Joes, Colorado
by Anita Mumm

NAVIGATION 38
by Claire Boyles

AJE (SCREENPLAY) 41
an excerpt
by Erin Harper and Erin Greenberg

ANIMAL ENCOUNTERS 59
Five Faunal Pieces Composed by Attendees of a Community Creative Writing Class Hosted by Anita Mumm
by anonymouses

DITCH DRIVING 68
by Maureen Hearty

EVERYTHING IS A CLOUD 72
by Nina Elder

THE IOWA SCHOOL FOR THE BLIND 74
excerpted from the novel Rise of the Haugenberrys
by Zach Boddicker

THE HIGH WINDS BLOW 81
excerpted from the forthcoming novella It Will Follow the Rain
by Emmett Wilder

THE GOAL IS TO DELIGHT YOURSELF 93
Eleven Prosodic Pieces Composed at a Community Writing Workshop Helmed by Claire Boyles
by anonymouses

THREE POEMS 115
by Andrea Moore

SUCCESSFUL ARTISTRY IN THREE PARTS 124
More Lessons in Failure
by Gregory Hill

PATTERNS OF THE PAST 147
A Brief History of Colcha Embroidery in Colorado
Trent Segura

The Authors & Artists 153

introduction

by Kirsten Stoltz, co-director of the Prairie Sea Project

At dusk, the rural landscape often feels like a dream, a place where one could float along aimlessly. We seek out places to anchor ourselves, hoping to learn, listen, and experience the alternative reality of rural America. Inspired by the geography of the high plains ecosystem, the Alma Creative Residency was founded to capture imaginative rural environments where human connection happens through sharing ideas, experiences, and relationships at the artists' own pace. Our goal is to offer time for wandering, discovery, imagination, and creation.

Artistic responses to and in rural places have been on the rise, with varying degrees of success. We have found that successful projects incorporate transformation, interaction, and are built through connection, learning, invitation, exchange, and collaboration. The artists featured in this volume have explored ideas about creating a living art that will grow and change in time, shaped and enhanced by their experiences in Joes, Colorado (population 75). Participants suggest the ever-changing moods of the sky, the transitory effects of light, weather, seasons, and the cycles of growth, decay, and death.

As Lucy Lippard wrote in 2007, "There is no reason to exaggerate the elusive power of art. Artists cannot change the world...alone. But when they make a concerted effort, they collaborate with life itself." As artists relinquish authorship of creativity and build a holistic vision for the future world, we gain knowledge and compassion. Prairie Sea Projects is an organization thoroughly invested in community building and dreaming. Our goal is to provide time and space for artists participating in the Alma Creative Residency program to find coexistence, build connections, and share the significance of the prairie environment that surrounds them.

The Alma residency artists generally make art that doesn't hang on walls, is often temporary, explores language, and incorporates ideas of relationships and co-creation. Public and private funding for this type of work and for rural organizations is significantly less than for urban ones. Additionally, as our communities shrink due to factors like school consolidation, failing businesses, and a lack of social infrastructure, we, in spite of limited resources, remain the only art programs in Northeastern Colorado. We can offer this residency thanks to the generosity of like-minded individuals: Lynn and David Gottmann, Laia Mitchell of The Gates Family Foundation, and the Arts in Society granting program. This core group of funders recognizes the power of creativity as integral to life itself and believes deeply that art can flourish in areas with sparse populations. They support artists in the purest of ways, offering them space to experiment, grow, and evolve as creative individuals.

Fundamentally built on reciprocity in exchange for room and board, we ask participants to engage with the community by building a shared creative expression. Formatted as art workshops, readings, meals, and gatherings, these events are deeply valued by individuals who are often marginalized in the art world. Artist Andrea Moore hosted a natural dye class that mirrored her residency exploring the experimental meadow growing at the Prairie Futures site. Writers Claire Boyles and Anita Mum led creative writing group exercises based on personal experiences in Joes and beyond. Each opportunity is an expression of shared experience, a way of finding ourselves in a cohort constructing new creative ideas inspired by the Colorado High Plains.

Maureen Hearty (Prairie Sea Projects co-director) and Teague von Bohlen capture small moments, building a vocabulary for rural assimilation through personal experiences. Their perspectives offer solutions for understanding small-town life and its functional landscape. Expanding this rural vernacular, author Zach Boddicker and novelist Emmitt Wilder craft a dystopian array of Eastern Colorado experiences, from roadside flag fanatics to new feelings about wind. Each contributes to a connection in Eastern Colorado, fostering a place for redefining rural life.

Artist Trent Segura Colcha's creations are inspired by place and the memories they hold. An uncommon practice outside the San Luis Valley, Colcha embroidery reimagines our world from macro to micro through imaginative perspectives, psychedelic thread movements, and the experience of home. Nina Elder found herself at the residency captivated by the sky, discovering a parallel between the constant atmospheric shifts and her own nomadic artistic journey. Similarly, filmmakers Erin Harper and Erin Greenwell offer a screenplay that explores ideas of new worlds and how we build understanding and connection along the way.

News outlet The Colorado Sun's Sunlit section has become a supporter in Colorado's emergent writers community. With our partner Kevin Simpson, co-founder of the Colorado Sun, we have built a successful one-week residency for MFA creative writing students. Writers (Anita Mumm, the 2023 awardee) are invited to Joes to write and create literary works, investing time and energy into their own future success.

Author Gregory Hill, ignites our imaginations and rebuilds places that need rebuilding. "Exchange your mouth for your ears" is a mantra outlined in his essay that perfectly describes the Alma Creative Residency program. The Prairie Sea Projects through this residency wants to change the culture of silos in the art world, break through the echo chamber, and listen. People are often-times afraid of silence and fill gaps with static—but stillness and quietness give us power and allow us to hear the land, the sky, the animals, and function as one ecosystem in a liminal space bidding time in rural Colorado.

once more to the rural

A Week in Joes, Colorado

by Teague von Bohlen

The one who plants trees, knowing that he will never sit in their shade, has at least started to understand the meaning of life.

Rabinranth Tagore

Forward

There had been no years, or so goes the refrain from E.B. White's seminal essay on time and yearning and mortality, "Once More to the Lake." That piece, originally published in a 1941 issue of *Harper's* magazine, recalled his return to a place of his youth—a Maine lakeside resort, where he was taken as a boy. It's a pilgrimage of sorts, and the religiousness of his faith in this place is central to the work, as White's imagined displacement between him and the son he's brought. His memories of being that boy battle with his reality; he finds himself out of time throughout the piece. *There had been no years.*

When I first encountered "Once More to the Lake," I didn't much care for it—but that had more to do with me being 17. I found it elegiac, something for which the young me had very little patience. Stories in general require a certain number of years lived to truly appreciate—or maybe as Indiana Jones famously quipped: it's not the years, it's the mileage. Either way, the appreciation of narrative beyond simple thrill requires some well-earned perspective; stories about mortality perhaps even more so.

But elegy is something to which I aspire now, at 53. Not in the sense of death, necessarily, though that is of course the end of any story, as Hemingway reminded us. But in terms of loss, which is much more profound an experience in the human condition, something we realize over and over again. Death is, mercifully, something we only occasionally see. Loss is something we endure every day, in small and large things. From a carelessly dropped mug that you've had and used for decades to a grandmother who quietly slips from the world while you're off in another town, in another life, and you go home to honor her and you watch for the wrens she loved and sit in the last chair in which she sat, and you buy her the popcorn she loved one more time, just because, and you pour it on the ground for her like Irish whiskey.

There's beauty in loss, of course, of course. This is not a

profound statement. It's inherent in all of the arts, in all our history, in all of who we are as people. We are both blessed and cursed by memory, because we lose something with each moment that passes. Mark the moment, right now, as you read this. That moment will never come back. Neither will this one. Or this one. It might seem like we're wasting time right now, you and I, but no moment is ever wasted. Not really. Loss isn't negative. It isn't positive. It just is. Time is neutronic, and so is its passing.

This is not news to rural America, where beginnings and endings are central to living. Planting to harvest, season to season, cloud to clear, rain to snow to drought and back again. The cycle, such as it is, is constant, even in its variation. This too shall pass, whatever this is.

And it was all of this that excited me about spending a week in Joes, Colorado, about witnessing a whole new and yet completely familiar place in the world. If there's one thing that I've learned from my past writings, especially my flash fiction collection *Flatland* (in which I collaborated with my brilliant cousin Britten Traughber, whose photography does much the same work chronicling and honoring the spirit of the Midwest), it's that the rural is remarkable and delicate and probably eternal, much like Maine lakes or whatever natural place in this world fills you up with something you can't really name, but that feeds you well nonetheless.

So forgive me my occasional lapse into the language of E.B. White and his "Once More to the Lake" as I go once more to the rural. It is very much on my mind as I sit here in this century-old farmhouse writing about the place and the people of the great plains, the patterns of life indelible, the fade-proof horizons, fields both fallow and full, the pastures unshatterable, the buffalograss and cottonwoods forever and ever, life all around, and utterly without end.

Teague von Bohlen
June 2023

Day One: Going Home to Somewhere I've Never Been

When I think of the rural parts of America, it's always summer. August, probably, because the crops are tall and the air is so thick that even the gnats fly in languid circles complaining about the heat. But in this temporary and yet somehow permanent world of full fields and shining sun, everything is right, because everything is in its place, everything is as it should be. You will sweat, but so is everyone. You will work, but so is everyone. You will complain like everyone, and then laugh at yourself for doing it like everyone, because as we all know here, there is no use in protesting what is. It's rule number one of living close to the land: you are only a part of it all. Not even a necessary one. There's beauty in that, and humility too, and it's possible that the one can't exist without the other.

I took myself to Joes, Colorado, because it had been too long since I'd had dirt between my toes. I'd been in the city too long again, gotten used to seeing weather as a minor detail in the day. I wondered how Joes would compare to the Midwestern towns I was used to—if it were really true that all small towns, all farm communities, all out-in-the-sticks environments were the same, all the same. It's a lesson I learned when I wrote my first novel, *The Pull of the Earth*, set in Moweaqua, Illinois, population somewhere-around-2000ish. I thought I'd been writing about my hometown, and I was and I wasn't. Readers from all over—Oregon, New York state, Florida, Arizona—said they recognized that town. That they were from there, too. It was my first lesson in the ubiquity of the rural, of the nature of living in nature, of there really being no years, and no distance either.

There's only so much you can learn about a place without

being there. You can find a bit about its history, though you know it's all whitewashed and prettied up. You can see its statistics, but you know too well that old line about lies and damn lies. You can see pictures, but in the end, photographs are someone else's experience of a thing. A beautiful one, to be sure. An edifying one, absolutely. Art, without a doubt. That's the value of an image: it's you seeing the world through someone else's window.

But to know a place yourself, you have to go. You have to be there. And with the invitation of the Prairie Futures project, an NEA-funded agricultural and art installation, that's what I did, live in Joes, Colorado for a week in June.

When I set out, I packed in everything I thought I might need. I overprepared, because that's what most of us do. I've always admired those few who can pack nearly nothing into a small backpack and just light out for the territories. I can't; I need to know where my fresh underwear is coming from tomorrow. I consider it a deficit of character: I imagine my forefathers taking nothing but a tank full of gas and a pack of smokes and a rolled-down window with them to wherever they wanted to go. I don't smoke, and my car is a hybrid electric, but I do keep the window down and the sun on my left arm.

The drive was exactly what I expected, a revelation of the familiar. Crops on both sides of an open road. Very little in the way of traffic or proof of human life. Half the folks I saw on the road were driving tractors very slowly. It was a reminder to me that things move at their own pace here, and if you don't get used to it, it will drive you crazy. I took a breath, geared down, reminded myself where I was.

Driving in the country isn't just relocation: it's transubstantiation. We become new people, people who wave at each other for no reason other than that they are nearby, passing us on a road without lanes going sixty. We salute them just for being; we recognize their presence and share a fleeting moment of community. *We are here*, that wave says. *We are the same, you and I. I see you.*

Being seen is a thing in the rural landscape, where so much is hidden by the tall grasses and whispering crops.

Between the bug splatter on my windshield and the roar of the air rushing past my open window, the drive was cathartic, like I was shedding the city with every mile, becoming this other me, one that didn't have to worry about traffic or noise or the hell that can be other people. Once I turned off I-70 and onto U.S. Route 36, I could have been anywhere in the heartland of America. I *was* anywhere in the heartland of America, because it's all the same, planted soil, fallow fields, murky culverts, windmills small and towering. And barns, which dot the landscape like tombstones, most of them no longer in service to anything except identifying this landscape as a place that once required them.

Driving in the rural parts of the country always makes me think of my own Grandma Rita and her sister, my great-Aunt Freda, who'd still talk about "the hard road." By that, they were referring to Illinois Route 51, which was established on what had been in their youth in the first quarter of the 20th century just another dirt and gravel farm road. While it was an operable metaphor at the same time, they certainly didn't mean it that way. Women of that generation had no time for metaphor. They would have considered that fancy, putting on airs. I remember sometimes being accused by both of them of being "windy," which came I think from being "full of wind" which in turn was a nicer way of saying I was full of something else.

As a child, it confused me that they still referred to 51 as the "hard road." But I accepted it as just a thing that was, like the stories of Grandma's first farmhouse not having electric or plumbing, of the place where my mother grew up not having air conditioning to fight the summer second-story swelter. It's a matter of perspective, I know: my grandmother remembers outhouses, I remember UHF, my own children cannot conceive how anyone ever lived without internet. And so it goes, binding us together and separating us at the same time.

It didn't take me long to get to Joes on northeastern Colorado's own hard road. Two hours and forty years ago or so is all.

Joes, Colorado is essentially a cluster of houses with Prairie Futures, a post office, and a liquor store, these days. According to the 2020 census, 82 people lived there, which was a 2.5% upswing from 2010, when only 80 officially called it home. There's an old grocery that's been closed since the early 1990s but still has its sign up, and the drapes in its front windows drawn. There are two motels on the east end of town, at one time servicing travelers on Route 36, now de facto storage units for the owners while they make their various plans for redemption. There have been restaurants: a Mexican joint that lasted a while, and an Amish-style place that apparently didn't. A machine shop for selling and servicing tractors and the like. A few churches, only one that's still open for worship. A communications company that's the lifeline to the rest of creation. There's a community center and a doctor's office that share the same wide gravel lot with the park, which is lovely and colorful and too poorly used. Liberty Elementary is right down 36, and to buy food or gas, you have to drive at least ten minutes. More, if you want options.

But small towns aren't about places; they're about people and time. If you've spent your life there, in the same places as your parents and theirs, you start to recognize the things you're doing for the first time and also as part of a larger cycle. You're in the middle of the simple act of frying an egg in butter and salt or walking through tall grasses and feeling the seed heads brush against your shin, and you're not you in that moment but your grandmother or your father or your many uncles doing that same thing. Different time, different skin, but all the same, all the same.

I arrived in Joes in the evening, as the sun was setting behind the old barn that squatted just to the West of where'd I'd be staying, in the second floor of that barn's equally-venerable farmhouse.

I unpacked a bit. I turned on the radio instead of the television. I lit a candle. I made myself at home.

Day Two: History and Where We Keep It

The second day of anything is all about exploration. The first is just arrival, resetting, enduring the move and re-planting yourself somewhere different. But come the next morning, you have to set out to see what there is to see. It's an instinct buried in us that's more about survival than adventure. The roaming is necessary: we have to see what the land has for us, and how we fit in.

Joes is a quiet place, almost always. The silence is punctuated by the occasional semi rumbling down 36. They don't even slow down. No real reason to. They say there are eighty-some people here, but they're not evident most of the time. Which makes sense. People don't walk around a town without any places to walk to.

Joes is like too many of America's small communities: inert dioramas of the place they used to be. The buildings along what passes for Main Street are boarded-up, little more than storage anymore, and not usually for the stuff connected to its own history. The old Alma Motel on the east side of town isn't replete with old bedframes and dressers, though there's some of that still haunting those old rooms. But a large part of what's contained within is the detritus of other stories, other owners, other uses. It's a hodgepodge of items not unlike what you might find in an old antique store, though the stuff is arguably of lesser monetary value. Through the windows, I see a mystifying collection of unrelated objects: an old nacho dispenser; a plastic bin full of old rotary phones; what looks to be a doctor's jacket, bone-white except for where someone has laid a greasy carburetor. Cushions to couches that aren't there. Pillows stacked and bound together with duct tape. A calendar on the wall, the date too dim to see in the dusty half-light. And more, of course. All things which look individually useful, maybe, or even collectible, if you squint. Which means they're kept, just in case. And the accidental hoard grows. There's room, so why not?

And it's not just the buildings. The land itself here is littered with beautiful old machinery. Cars, trucks, tractors, combines, motorcycle parts and various engines, pump parts and signage. It's almost like a crop in rusted browns and reds nestled in the June green of weeds not yet dried. They appear in piles that give off the aura of purpose; it seems clear that someone put this shell of a 1951 Chrysler Windsor up against a couple of small trees and never came back for it. It ended up being parted out, purposefully or not, piece by piece. Vegetation grew up around it, weaved into it, locking it in place. The tires gave up the fight and flattened at some point. Kids smashed the windows, tore out the seats. A cat died in the back, now nothing but bone and fur. Weather did the rest.

But it was someone's dream, this car. Someone picked it off a lot at least once, drove it home, showed it off, had their picture taken in front of it, maybe leaning back on the hood and crossing their arms. It carried people, and people carried stories, in and out, to and from. Its sticker price in '51 was $2400 give or take, about $30K in today's money. A year's salary, probably, especially for a small farmer. Why and when was this gorgeous old sedan parked here and left? Anyone's guess. And that mystery is part of the joy in its discovery.

The huge old barn I saved for another day. It was right there, a short walk away from my door, and I have to admit, there was a bit of saving-the-best-for-last about it too.

But I did plumb the depths of what looked like an abandoned house across 36. I'd find out later that it had been a meth lab in the shell of an old church, decades ago. I was assured that if I googled it, I'd find out more about it, but no number of Boolean searches turned up anything at all. The history of Joes is a secret well-kept, primarily because most of it isn't written down. It lives in the heads and memories of those that lived here, that still live here, and more stories are lost with every heart that stops beating. Loss, again.

The abandoned place was porchless, concrete steps leading up to an empty frame floor in front of a missing front door. But through where that door should have been shone light from the back; the entire rear of the house looked to be wide open too. So I doubled around. There wasn't much left. The floor was gone; you could see along the walls where it had been. There had been a basement, I assumed, from the single low window under the floor line. However deep the basement had at one time been, it was now full of the charred and rotting remains of whatever was here when the fire started. There were still scraps of drapery on that window, the once-brightly-colored 60s or 70s fabric now bedraggled and heavy with unclean, but still there clinging to its thin rod.

Scattered throughout the house, in the dirt and detritus and the chemical remnants of the meth lab that took it all, there were still small treasures waiting to be found. This is how I know there can't be that many teenagers living in Joes: most of it was untouched. Not that a bored fifteen year old would find most of it interesting: there was a plastic grocery bag with John Philip Sousa CDs stacked inside. A golden trophy with a crawling baby atop it that was awarded to someone for winning 2nd Prize in the "Prince" category. A fast-food Batman. A 1983 game board from something called ALLOWANCE. A waterlogged box with stacked glass ashtrays and a desklamp missing its shade, with a flattened carton of what used to hold 30-watt bulbs wedged over the top, perhaps in some wan gesture of protection. There was more, too: broken tile and dishware, unidentifiable fabrics in filthy irregular strips, soda cans and cigarette butts (there are the kids, finally).

Everything here was a question. What happened the last night before the fire? How did it start? When was the last time someone was happy here? What marriages happened inside these walls, what baptisms, what funerals? What faith bounced audibly off that half-broken ceiling? What kids ran around in the back, still wearing their church clothes, frantic to stop singing and play? What potlucks were held here, and what dishes were the favorite? What church was it? What did they believe? What made it close? What did it become, and how, and how fast? What happened?

Don't bother searching for the answers. Someone knew them, and they're either gone, or not talking. All we're left with are questions and buildings packed with stuff that tell stories, but the wrong ones.

Day Three: Weather

It rumbled last night, clouds thumping against each other in the utter darkness of the plains.

I got up early. I often fantasize about the inherent nobility of the workaday sunrise, in the misty morning when even a day doomed to be sweaty will start out with a chill. In these dreams, I'm gassing up my truck, heading off into a day of labor, which is where that particular dream usually ends, because as romantic as it might be, that moment of visible breath and Carhartt jackets and gas fumes and coffee, the back-breaking nature of the real work that follows is less so.

Both my grandfathers were farmers. I feel like I don't know enough about what they did, about their daily toils and all they had to know. I know enough to understand that running a farm is like running your own little world; you're gambling every day, betting against the house. You're hedging that you can plant enough, tend enough, care enough, survive enough, keep your fingers crossed enough that the soil will put forth a bounty such that you and yours can live and thrive and harvest in the Fall in order to do it all again come Spring. That much, I know. But the intricacies of that life—the daily victories and disappointments, the ability to weather a bad year among the good and keep going, the trick to turn over a diesel engine that's sputtering in the dank cold of a springtime dawn—those things I don't. I have become soft. I work with my hands, but on lettered keys. My weeding is done on Saturday mornings before it gets hot. What I grow, I grow for aesthetics, not for food, not for survival, even if a little beauty is necessary for that, too.

It's a holy thing, waking yourself up with the sun, a matter of faith that this is where you're supposed to be at exactly that time and outside of time too. Everything is a gesture of invocation; there is potential in each breath. It is standing at the kitchen window and looking outside onto the world. It is getting behind the wheel and pausing for that one delicious second as you rest into the driver's seat before turning the key in the ignition. It is the smell of dawn, the evaporation of dew. The song of unseen birds. The fickle breeze that promises to stay when you know it won't. The sun that's only begun its work. And so have you.

Time is irrelevant to weather. The two exist right next to each other, but they're feuding uncles who don't speak. Rain is rain, no matter the years. Thunder never sounds different. Lightning still strikes, and mud still cakes. Getting wet is still humbling, still worthy of comment, like the clouds have once again gotten one over on you, that for all our inventiveness as a species we still haven't discovered any better response to a sudden shower than just going inside. Escape is our only avenue, and that's something the rural knows all too well.

How do you fight a tornado? By sending everything you love to the cellar. A snowstorm? By stocking food, filling the tub with fresh water, making sure you have candles and batteries and blankets. Flooding? Go upstairs and pray. Drought? Prayer again, this time with a dry throat.

We are at the mercy of every whim of the skies. Those living outside the cities know this in their bones. It's etched into them like tree rings, taught by example and hard experience and stories like the one where the pastor of a nearby church was taken away by a twister while attempting to corral his dogs, and was never found, just disappeared as though he'd ascended, his own personal Rapture, and people still talk about it like that because it's easier to think about, kinder both to them and his memory too, than to consider that his last moments were nothing but terror and wind and pleading and sudden shrapnel made from a world that was recognizable only moments before.

This is the world into which we awake every day, no matter the work ahead of us, no matter the forecast. We get up and we keep our head down, just in case. We work, and watch the skies.

Day Four: Gatherings

I went to another small town nearby on my fourth day in Joes—this time a little community called Vernon, which a friend had assured me these days was little more than a ghost town. And they had a point, I thought as I pulled onto what still served as Main Street, even if it had about as much as Joes seemed to. A liquor store that also served as a post office and quick stop, so long as all you wanted was canned soda and candy bars. An impressively large central park that looked mostly unused. A smattering of homes both in-use and clearly not. Farms encroaching. No one in sight but a pre-teen in a Broncos jersey on a riding mower.

The difference between Vernon and Joes seemed to be that Joes hadn't torn down most of its buildings. At least that's the case according to the gentleman I spoke to briefly while checking out the store to see what there was to find out. As always, the lesson was this: if you want to know something in a farm community, look for the guy in the feed cap.

He said he'd been living in Vernon all his life, farming, seen a lot of changes through the years. Talked about how it used to have a lot going on—its own bank, two grocery stores, even a movie theater. Over time, it all closed. "Not much here now," he said, before asking me what I was doing asking. Conversation is the commerce in places like this: he's my story, I'm his, and so the pattern repeats. It's always been the same. I didn't ask for his name, and he didn't ask for mine. We knew each other's credentials all we needed to. I asked what he remembered about the town, and he said it wasn't really a town anymore. It was just a "gathering of houses."

I should have asked him more, but he answered what questions I did pose with as few words as possible, and I took his laconic approach as an expression of the limits of his patience. So I set out on my own, walking around the perimeter of the grassy park that bullseyed what amounted to the whole of the town, and making my way over to the only other non-residential structure other than the little multipurpose store. It was a school—looked like it could still be in use from a distance. But as I got closer, it was clear that it was not. The gate on the front door was locked. The playground on the east side fell apart more and more the closer I walked to it. The windows were either boarded up or showed the same sort of storage-use as the ones down in Joes.

There's a little bit about Vernon School on the History Colorado website, but not nearly enough. It was built in 1927, and boasted an impressive gymnasium addition from 1949, its classic varnished floor, stacked bleachers, and old scoreboard crowning its regulation-size basketball court. Yuma County history claims it was one of the first of that size in the area, which must have been a thing for this town in the 1950s. Looking through the gym windows is like looking through a time tunnel, like a team wearing white cotton togs could jog out dutifully at any moment, girls in lettered shirts and skirts cheering along the baseline, a crowd fresh from their fields cheering on the home team. Kids with pennants and popcorn. The booster club selling pop and candy. It all still echoes there.

And it has to; the school itself was closed in 1969, which is remarkable both in terms of its preservation as well as for me personally. I was born in August of the same year. The school had been shuttered for just barely longer than I've been alive, and yet it's still here, still looking like a game could happen, like a crowd could appreciate something like a regulation-size court, the squeaks of rubber soled shoes and the blaring horn of time running out still ringing in my ears.

If the school looked timeless, a close inspection of the playground decidedly did not. The apparatuses of childhood activity have changed radically since the Vernon School had these installed, probably in the 50s or 60s by the look. Everything was made of metal. A thin slide with very little in the way of rails on the way up or on the way down. A swingset with grid-iron seats that probably weighed as much as the kid sitting on it and waffling the skin of his backside. The obligatory empty tetherball pole. The bars-upon-bars jungle gym inset into an asphalt pad. A splintery teeter-totter once painted green. And of course the merry-go-round, at one time every kid's invitation to learn about centrifugal force the hard way.

There wasn't much more to see in Vernon. I took the driving back slowly so as to savor the Saturday afternoon. Later on, there was a gathering of a whole other kind in Joes, a marketplace of food and music and neighbors coming together to spend the evening sharing it all. It was as lovely as it sounds like it should be, a few guys with guitars, a food truck with some of the best burgers a body is like to have, all in a garden area and a community pavilion made for just this purpose. The mosquitos couldn't keep people away, though they tried.

I don't know how the party would have ended had it not been for the storm that came up. The skies had been threatening all night, the topic of many a conversation, but the hope was that it would pass. The company was too good, the burgers too fat, the music too familiar and friendly and fine. But still it came, that first wave of humidity and insistent wind like a guitarist's chatter before they pluck the first string, softening up the crowd with a hint of what's to come. Then there's one gust that's like a premonitory chord, something that signifies that there's been a point of no return reached, and then there comes the first blazing brightness of lightning against a black sky, and even the guy with the guitar sees that it's time to pack it up, get in out of it as the foretold gods grin and lick their chops in the hills. The scattering, the grabbing, the regrouping. Get a tarp on the amp. Close the shutter on the food truck. Are the kids in the truck? Unplug everything. Put the instruments away. It was time for the sky to sing, and for us all to listen.

Maybe it's the only way for a gathering to end, by way of the surrounding world deciding that it's time. Once and for all, despite the hangers-on, consequences immaterial, it's over. We don't get to decide; we only get to respond.

Day Five: Dead Islands and Silent Circles

When my grandparents on my mother's side moved into town and out of the old farmhouse on the rural road a few miles out, they did so almost as one leaves a highway motel. Pack up your clothes, get ready to go, check out and close the door behind you.

They brought more than just clothing, of course—dishes and kitchen stuff, photo albums, the cookie-jar-owl, the color-swirled glass-ball paperweights that went on the coffee table, my grandfather's pipe stand, the bedding, the good furniture. Everything else that had been in the house was carted down into the cellar, a dirt-floor space that was only in use for tornados and jarred bread-and-butter pickles. Nothing was boxed up; it was stacked or dumped into piles. By the time the house was empty, the cellar was full.

And then they tore down the house and buried the cellar under the topsoil.

It was almost like a sacrifice to an agricultural deity of some sort, one that appreciates out of date upholstery and toys the kids don't play with anymore. The idea has fascinated me since I was a child and first heard of this happening. For one, it's made me hang on to things more—for better and for worse. Not in that "I grew up in the Depression" way that excuses itself, but in the sense of "wow, does our family have like *no* history?" I would watch *Antiques Roadshow* and marvel at how these people still had their maternal great-great grandmother's sideboard that was made of planks from the hull of the USS Constitution. I have my great-grandmother's chicken fork. The fork she used to flip her fried chicken in the pan. This is my legacy. (*Antiques Roadshow*, I'm in the book.)

But it makes sense. My grandma was never one to take part in the romance of things. Objects were utility to her, and nothing more. She had a few favorite objects—placeholders for memories of family, etc. That cookie-jar owl came from her mother's kitchen. She had some Fostoria from some aunts, a modest collection that she'd added to here and there. Who knows—that chicken fork might have come from generations before, but if so, that story fell away from the world when she did.

More important than my minor hoarding instincts is my interest in what lies beneath. That's not necessarily a metaphor, though I suppose that it's that too. But literally: what's buried only inches under the earth? What's behind that barn wall? What's slipped through the cracks of this splintered wood floor? What's in the attic, what's in the basement, what's in the old motel that's been locked up along a mostly abandoned state highway since the 1970s? Everything above ground made me wonder what lay under it, in it, hidden not by purpose but by impatience and necessity and time.

Time again. It comes up over and over here, because there is and there isn't. Everything I've written so far about my grandparents' farmhouse and its interring into the earth has been about time. But their ambivalence to objects is very much evidence of time's immaterial nature. Where time is meaningless, so is nostalgia. You can't miss what you never cared for, or thought about.

Not that such a thing isn't remarkable: my grandfather used to remark on these sites of old homesteads out in the fields all the time. You can see them everywhere on farm roads: gravel drives leading off over a diversion pipe so the ditch can flow. The gravel peters out as it crosses that culvert threshold, ending in a ring of vegetation and foundation and construction remnants of various types. Sometimes there's a lone staircase or what used to be a chimney. Sometimes you can still see the concrete pad, or at least identify where it sits under too-little airbrushed topsoil. It's a patch of wild in a carefully cultivated field, an anomaly in a careful plan of agricultural attack.

My grandpa called them Dead Islands, and I wish he were still around for me to ask in what way he meant that. I'd like to think he meant of them in some way of remembrance of the people that had at one time—probably for a long time—called it home, eked out a life there, sweated in the summers and froze in the winter snow. Raised dogs and children and sometimes a little hell, family-style, something that includes firecrackers and watermelon and lightning bugs.

But he probably meant it in that farmer's way of it being a useless piece of land for growing crops. Too expensive to clear, and too jumbled a mess to plant. So there it sits, this tombstone of a rough quarter-acre, still taking up space but at least no longer requiring upkeep, power lines, septic. It endures because it is just troublesome enough.

Everything out here is measured in levels of troublesome, from the low end of "I'll get around to it someday" to "we gotta hop on that right now." If it's not an emergency, it's probably not on the itinerary. There are always more pressing matters.

This is the way children recognize their place in rural communities: they are expected not to be high on the list of things to which to be tended. It's not so much that they're expected to be seen and not heard, though that's a line you're bound to hear still to this day. It's that silence is just one strategy for not being a problem, and not being a problem is your duty because there are so many other problems that need solving.

For some, that responsibility for quiet becomes too much. They act out, ruin churches with meth, crash their Harley on a curve, joyride in the farm truck, climb the corn crib, drink out in the field when the crops are tall enough to hide everything. Even these acts of rebellion are sufficiently quelled by their own consequences: pregnancy, marriage, death, or relocation. The former two require the eventual acquiescence of the quiet, of finding one's place in the silent wheel. The latter are mute only in absence. But the quiet wins out, every time.

For others—for me—becoming part of the hushed system was opportunity to watch how it all worked. The pistons pumping, each one a person doing their part to keep the machine whirring, producing, moving, moving, moving ever forward, until that day when it's time to start again, tear it apart from siding to frame to foundation, push everything into a new under-earth home, cover it up in darkness and dirt like it was never there. To keep your voice low. To watch the dead islands rise.

Day Six: The Almost-There

I wasn't enough. That's the end-worry of living in the rural, out where your fate depends largely on an infrastructure and a maintenance and a gumption that we have to bootstrap ourselves. I'd call it anxiety, but that word itself is a citified concept. Not that it doesn't exist out here. It most certainly does. But it's an ever-present, not generally a thing about which to talk with someone. Not your spouse, not your kids, not your friends, certainly not a therapist. Therapy out here, where it exists, generally comes courtesy of some church, and most of them fully subscribe to the divine Sisyphean predicament as baseline. Always falling just short of the goal is the lesson directly from the Garden of old scripture. It's a story with countless faces. Whatever the mythoi, we are none of us allowed to stay.

It's the wrong lesson, even according to most of the Christian doctrine that pervades the rural parts of this country. That version of the story is more about forgiveness and the fealty that must follow, accepting Christ into your heart where he can set up camp, string a hammock between arteries and put his feet up. The Jesus I imagined growing up Methodist was a guy whose feet always hurt. Maybe I was just sensing how tired he must be. First crucifixion, and then millennia of being misunderstood insofar as love and acceptance and service to the world and everyone in it? Brutal.

But this isn't about religion, or the politics of it. We have enough of that, whole news stations devoted to preaching to the choir. This is about the rural parts of the world always striving for something that they know they'll never reach in this life. Religious faith is only one example of that, and given the assurances that clergy and doctrine alike provide, probably not the best one. But it serves as both homespun panacea and gathering element for a portion of the community, and in that, it has immense value.

Still we divide ourselves. It's what humans do, tribalism. In extreme cases, it's a terrible force, unifying within by destroying without. But when it's on a small scale, there's a smiling rivalry there. We laugh at each other's foibles. The Methodists chuckle about the Lutherans having to sing everything. The Lutherans rib the Baptists for putting eggs in the potato salad. The Baptists don't joke, but do comment that everyone else sure seems to have time to do it. And so it goes.

Sports in a small town is perhaps the best example of this: identification with a mascot and a school is a powerful drive throughout rural America. Where I grew up, there are sedimentary layers of local sports fans: the kids, who cheer for the local Raiders in their black and red; the middle-aged, who remember when the old high school teams were disbanded during consolidation, the old giving way to the new; and the old-timers, who still wear the yellow-and-blue insignia of the Indians team, a noble profile now sullied by perspectives they don't understand. That Native American profile insignia used to be emblazoned on the water tower. Now it's only on sweatshirts that you can't wear outside of town, and that embarrass the grandkids.

Joes, like many towns in rural America, had its moment in sports history. It happened all the way back in 1929, when an upstart team from Joes High School soundly thrashed Fort Collins HS 37 to 14 in the All-Colorado State Championship game in Greeley. Joes High School at the time was comparably tiny: the whole school, including all 12 grades, was often less than sixty students. Despite the team's coach never having played the game himself—he learned the rules from a book!—the team had already beaten state juggernauts like Denver's East High (whose fans complained about their loss to the small-town team, blaming the tiny facilities). From that state win, the Joes team would go on to the national playoffs in Chicago, where they'd fight off a number of teams from all over the country, eventually earning the 3rd Place Trophy that still sits in the Liberty High School gym. (The whole story is told in Nell Propst's 1987 book *The Boys from Joes*, now out of print—a good read, if you can find a copy.)

And here it is again: the almost-there. It's branded into the flank of rural America, limitless possibility that never sees fruition. The chase of something larger than ourselves. A yearning. It's what drives any faith, religious or otherwise. The promise of something better. It's why we go to school. It's why we date. It's why we marry. It's why we bring children into the world. Its why we work the world itself, crafting it in small ways all around us over and over again, season after season, despite the fact that the turning of time takes it all apart every winter. We hide our acorns like a squirrel hoard. We build it up knowing it will all fall.

Because the building—the act of creation without regard for

its longevity—is the point. The *entire* point. This is the thing the rural teaches us, the thing we forget in the rumbling insistence of a cityscape. That it's not product, but process. The means have little to do with their end. The world teaches us that the ends will take care of themselves; that the small bit we've carved out of this world—hopefully with some kindness and grace—will rise and fall. Everything returns to the earth, everything dissolves away, nothing gold can stay. It's the now that means something.

The sheer brightness of that is like the dizzying brilliance of a noonday sun. There, blindingly evident right above our heads. We have no need to look at it, or even consider it. We know it's there. We can feel it on our necks.

Day Seven: Exodus

Leaving isn't hard. Staying—now that's sometimes the challenge. Especially to the rural areas of this country, including most of northeast Colorado, as it sees its populations dwindle over time. Kids grow up and leave, heeding the siren call of the rest of the world, that kernel of productive dissatisfaction in the known, the inborn motivation to set out for the horizon and see what's there. Some come back. Too many don't.

And older folks pass on, despite their devotion to remaining. With all their knowledge of the inner workings of the world, the peccadillos of the ecosystem, the rules and regs, reasonable or not, they too go, taking it all with them. The ones left behind will wonder if they asked the right questions, asked them enough. They will know they didn't.

But the land remains, oblivious to the whims and cries of the people that make a home there. A patch of dirt doesn't care if it's a dead island or a bounty crop. It does its thing and marks the time and shakes its ancient head at the strange things we do with it, on it, in it, from it. Whether we come together as a community or we don't; whether we till the soil or we leave it be; whether we're planting crops or interring our dead. The rain will fall in Spring, the heat will bake in summer and cool in autumn and sleep under the snow in the winter before it wakes. Everything else is just detail, like the objects upon which we place arbitrary value, like the things we bury, like what we choose to call home. These are not absolutes. Their value exists only through our own eyes, and the land here, for all it witnesses, is blind.

I was almost gone too. My week was up. I'd saved the barn for the end of my trip like other people might savor the last M&M in the bag. I'm a sucker for old barns—grew up in and around them, especially the old white hulk of a thing that squatted on the road-side-edge of my aunt and uncles place when I was in half-day kindergarten and would spend every afternoon there. My cousin and I would spelunk the old barn—not in use by then for years, maybe decades—even though we weren't supposed to. Probably especially because we weren't supposed to; prohibition has never been anything other than inherent challenge. The sliding doors on the front were chained and padlocked, but also swung out just enough at the bottom for two determined five-year-olds to belly-crawl our way inside.

There are rules about old barns. One, there are always mice. Two, there is either an owl in the rafters or one that will return shortly. Three, everything shifts, so step with care. Four, everything you see will seem to have more value than it actually does once you take it out into the sunlight. Five, there will be sounds to which you cannot confidently ascribe origin. Six, there are ghosts everywhere. Seven, this is their place, so remember yours.

I'd heard that people were trying to save this barn, recognize it as the landmark building that it is and deserves to be seen as, preserve it for later generations and be able to use it for the community that it was built to serve. Money is the issue, of course; money and someone's time. It's a footrace now, between the human instinct to tell a story and the juggernaut schedule of entropy. Everything falls, yes, yes. *But if*...we say in chorus, to which the reply is always: everything falls, yes, yes. Another life cycle in a land full of them. With enough capital, we can preserve the barn in Joes. For now.

Shelves of things have a certain draw to them. Objects, tools, things set aside for a now-lost purpose. They all take on the same color, all become a rusty palette of earth colors as they progress on their slow descent. I pawed through what I could reach, mindful not to stir the barn owl that was indeed above me, rustling suspiciously. I balanced, shaking, on a paint-flaked solid-core door seesawed over a four-stroke engine block on top of a yellow highway sign denoting a winding road up ahead, stretching to reach what I thought might be the swiss-cheesed metal seat of an old John Deere. And then I stopped. I didn't know how secure my footing was, didn't need to see that seat any more closely, wouldn't know what to do with it if I had it in my hands. I had explored enough.

I packed up my car in silence, taking in the last sounds of the landscape in Joes. It sounded the same as it had when I arrived: wind and birds, a far-off engine thrumming, the occasional car hurtling by on highway 36. This may be a place where there seems to be no years, but time is a thing, and imposes its requirements on us all. We live through, we age out, we are born, live our allotted days, and then pass. We come and we go, and we hope to be recalled as kind.

These are the things that stay.

It's like what my new Joes friend Gary said to me several times while he was showing me around town: "Things are always changing, but nothing's different". And he was right. They could put that on any town sign in America. It would ring true anywhere.

the oasis

Seven Lives in Joes, Colorado

by Anita Mumm

This past July, I had the privilege of spending a week in Joes as a writer-in-residence, sponsored by Prairie Sea Projects and *The Colorado Sun*. I grew up in western Kansas and had been through Joes many times to visit relatives in Denver, and later as a Coloradan going the opposite direction to visit my family. I had no idea what gems were hidden just out of sight from the highway.

During my time at the Alma Creative Residence, I read books, took walks, met people from the community, and taught a creative writing workshop. All the while, I was surrounded by beauty: works of art, wildflower gardens, epic thunderstorms, and magnificent sunsets. Joes was a creative sanctuary for me, and that got me thinking about the other creatures who make a home there, whether for a day or a night or an entire life. This piece imagines a peek into the heads of seven nonhuman residents I encountered (or might have if I had stayed just a little longer).

1/ Male redwing blackbird trills from a juniper tree at dawn

Ahem. Mee, mee, mee, do-re-mi, ahem.
JOYFUL, JOYFUL, WE ADORE THEE...

Kidding! We feathered kin have no need to borrow from human hymns, which are in fact crude plagiarisms of our own much longer-standing musical traditions. Now then:

Greunnk greeleeleeeeunnnk
Click, cheep, chickareeeee
Greunnk konkareeeee
Click, cheep, chickareeeeeee!

2/ Monarch butterfly lands on a milkweed in the Prairie Gardens

Glory be! A jungle of life-giving Motherplants. Wait 'til I tell the gals in Michoacán[1]. Found our springtime nursery! Even I was beginning to doubt myself. All those miles of dust and tumbleweeds...infernal drought. Thought I'd never make it. But finally, sustenance! Sunflowers, goldenrod, prairie coneflowers, and...be still my antennae—Is that a California poppy? Sweet nectar of the gods! Just a sip—just one sip!—and I'll be on my way.

Pardon? Of course, I can still fly straight. After all I've been through, and you judge?

Oh, swirling kaleidoscopic rainbows! A thousand shimmering sunrises! Up, up, and away, I go. To infinity, and...!

Which way is south? I'll follow the rainbow. Here I come, my flock! You thought I was lost. Never! Only 3,672,417 wingflaps to go.

*3/*Three horses whip flies with their tails in a pasture in the hot afternoon sun. The littlest one, an aging Shetland pony

And as I was saying, where is that blasted woman with the bag of carrots? The one who parks her rusting truck and comes walking across the road. Haven't seen her in days. Where is she, Mabel? With my carrots.

—Yes, dear, sorry dear. Absolutely. I couldn't agree more.

I can't survive another abandonment, Mabel. Remember the little girl? With the midnight eyes and the silken fingers she would run along my nose. Light as a feather, she was, when she climbed on my back. Where did she go? Why would she leave me? *Mabel,* are you listening?

—Yes, dear, sorry, dear. Very oppressive, indeed. And yet this, too, shall pass, will it not? All in good time, Henry, and so on and so forth.

Listen to you, Mabel. Going on and on as if you even heard what I said. You never, ever listen. Then you say you're sorry but you're not. You're not sorry at all. Isn't that right, Jasper?

~Now, Henry, you know quite well I don't take sides. That I find you both quite right generally. We're in this together, after all...in this confined space together...always together, day after day, year after year, decade after...Ouch! What have I said about the nipping, Henry?

The little girl used to call me gallant. Gallant, Jasper! But of course, *you* wouldn't know gallant if it slapped you on the rump.

4/Sunflower, growing from a fissure in the cement, leans out from the shade of the post office in late afternoon

Mighty Sun-god, supreme giver of life, I praise you!

But might you, just this once, perhaps this very evening, give over your place in the sky to the jealous thunder-gods? Those wrathful beings with their flashing eyes and terrible, growling bellies. Their power pales before your steady, beneficent smile. And yet, to have just one small drink. One small drink to lift these withered leaves to the heavens, that I may exalt you once more!

Please? Amen.

5/ Bat flies over Joes at dusk, bound for his favorite hunting ground—the blazing neon sign in front of the Plains Telephone Company

Oh, joy! What bounty awaits me tonight...Mosquitoes? Without a doubt. But so much work to eat enough of them. Lacewings! Scrumptious, delicate creatures. Rain beetles. Big, fat, oh-so-ripe June bugs—a must. There's one now! Crunchy on the outside, gooey center. De-*mmph-mmph*-licious.

Ah, but still I wait, for the holy grail of hunts. The feast of feasts. Giant of giants. You know the one—surely you do? The famed *Hyalophora cecropia*[2]. Oh, blessed night, were I to encounter one. Inch for inch and ounce for ounce, my equal. In beautiful combat we would swirl and spiral, up, up, into the night. We hang for a moment against the stars, quaking. Then down, down, down in a tangle of wings we plummet. A final glorious tailspin. Who wins? I cannot say. But what a marvelous way to go!

*6/*Coyote trots down a gravel road at dusk

Vigilant, vigilant. Danger here, danger there, anywhere, everywhere. Firesticks, poison, jagged metal jaws, lights that blind and freeze you in place. bang! snap! roooaar! Lose a paw, lose an eye, lose a tail, lose your life. But not me, o-ho, not me! Not today, not tomorrow. I am the clever one, the trickster, the dancing, dodging, disappearing shadow. The one who survives. Danger, danger, anywhere, everywhere. Ah, but the feast is worth it. Fat little hens, all in a row. Fast asleep and dreaming. So easy to slip under the fence. Easy to nudge open the flimsy door. Easy to reach up so very quietly and take my pick from the roost. Easy as—

Boom. What was that? Footsteps. One human male barks something to another. Sounds coming closer, closer... run, RUN!

7/Young raccoon leans out from behind a trash can, keeping watch. She turns back to her two masked companions, one balanced on top of the other

Careful, numbskulls! You almost tipped it over.

—Eeeeasy, sis. You worry too much. Have you ever seen us mess this up? Wait, don't answer that, lol.

~LOLOL. She has a point, bro. But seriously, we got this. Just a little higher and I can reach. Oooh, I smell pizza. Pepperoni and anchovies. Dash of tabasco, if I had to guess. Jackpot!

—Ow! That was my eye, dimwit.

Hurry up, you two. You'll wake that fool of a blue heeler. Like last time?

—You promised to stop bringing that up! Totally not our fault. Circumstances. Dumb luck.

~Could've happened to anyone!

Sssssshhht. Guys, what was that noise? Holy bullfrogs, there goes Coyote! I don't think he saw us. But whatever scared him is right behind...

—CRASH—

Now you've done it! Let's get out of here.
Mooooooove!

Just for Fun

When you're outside on a lunch break or an evening walk, what animals and plants do you come across? What can you imagine about their world and their ways? As you walk, maybe your dog stirs up a pheasant from the ditch—what are the two of them thinking in that moment of encounter? What might they say? A moment later, adrenaline floods your body as you nearly step on a bull snake crossing your path. But which of you is the most startled? What is the experience like from the snake's point of view? What is the red-tailed hawk thinking as she whirls in lazy circles far above you? What are the words to the meadowlark's song?

You can write a scene or story, or simply use this prompt to daydream. Let your imagination roam!

---

1. Monarch butterfly caterpillars have just one food source: the milkweed plant. In the fall, adult monarchs migrate to central Mexico, where they overwinter before returning north to lay their eggs in the spring.
2. The cecropia is the largest native moth in North America, with a wingspan of up to seven inches. Have you been lucky enough to spot one of these red, white, and brown beauties?

navigation

by Claire Boyles

The dry shrubland trails of the Rocky Mountain foothills demand a certain downward concentration. Rattlesnakes curl on the trail's edge. The jagged rocks could break an ankle. I don't often see the mountain lions, but they leave tracks. Most trails are so familiar that I don't carry a map. So familiar I sometimes forget to look up at the subtle changes in the landscape—varying shades of green after spring rains and summer monsoons, the birdsong shifts of avian migration, cumulus clouds, anvil clouds, mammatus.

As a new wilderness volunteer for the United States Forest Service, I am patrolling less familiar trails at higher altitudes. I might have to give a precise location to a search and rescue crew or make notes of exactly where a tree has fallen across a trail, so I signed up for the map and compass class, just as a refresher. I've spent plenty of time in the backcountry, and I thought I knew enough about maps.

Middle age can be an embarrassing stage of life, and not just because the term "midlife crisis" only ever describes ridiculous behaviors. I do enjoy a certain confidence I didn't have before, which makes it awkward to be confronted with things I think I know but don't, like how to get my bearings with a compass. Luckily, middle age has also come with a higher tolerance for discomfort and an expansive self-acceptance, and both facilitate humility.

Our instructor, Gerry, showed us how to align the compass with magnetic north, and then we took bearings by pointing the directional arrow at a notable landmark—reservoirs, seeps, visible peaks, jagged ridgelines. We added eight degrees to the number on the housing to get the magnetic declination, which accounts for the wandering North Pole.

Many people know about the wandering North Pole, but it was news to me. Turns out it moves around 55 kilometers a year. Toward Siberia. Inexplicably faster all the time.

Once we had bearings down, we hiked about a half mile up the trail. Gerry passed each of us a map and asked, *Where are we?* It was a moment of disconnect. I knew the trailhead, the trail name, and distance traveled. I knew exactly where I was. And I didn't. We learned to triangulate our position by taking bearings from three landmarks (being able to identify these landmarks in life and on maps is, Gerry says, our own due diligence) and drawing lines through each point. Eventually, with patience, all my lines crossed right where they should.

Mostly, I like getting older, not that I have any choice in the matter. But it has been disorienting to wander the familiar trails of my life as this new person I've grown into, and it's complicated by the fact that my landmarks have shifted. I left my teaching job to become a writer. I lost my father to cancer. My children are leaving home. My husband and I, married twenty-four years, are struggling in ways we did not expect. I am certain the pandemic has not made any of this easier.

. . .

I've been feeling a bit lost, and I'm grateful for this new, deeper way of knowing where I am and how to find myself, something I don't think I would have appreciated at any other stage of my life. My bearings are getting more accurate the more I practice them, though Gerry told me not to worry about being perfect. *You just have to be close enough that the search party can rescue you*. This was the most important takeaway from the class, reinforcing what I already knew—the people I love would come if I needed them, which means I'm still in the right place, or at least, I'm close enough.

aje (screenplay)

an excerpt

by Erin Harper and Erin Greenberg

During our Alma residency, Erin Greenwell and I immersed ourselves in the High Plains setting: the forever horizons, prairie grass, animal herds, undisturbed wild animal sounds, and the present-day site of the Battle of Beecher Island. This setting inspires the eight-episode (for now) series, Aje (working title), that we continue to write and develop.

During the week-long residency, Erin and I wandered for miles, met locals, and visited museums. Along the way, we filmed (Super Eight and digital) and wrote a half-hour pilot.

The following is a sneak peek of developmental materials for development labs, grants, and pitches:

- The scenes are excerpts from the end of the pilot. The first scene begins moments after a battle re-enactment has gone wrong.
- The images depict our footage. Some frame stills are collaged with inspired images by Sally Mann, Sara Wiles, Lauren Justice, and Lukas Avendano.

Aje Summary

Aje is a fantasy-fable connecting a bloodline of women over 200 years, starting with the last so-called "Indian War" fought near the blasted outpost town of Aje set on the brutal High Plains. This town will pass from birth to death under the vast, indifferent sky as "advanced" civilization tamps out its light through predation and depravity. But one mother line, whose women blend with the wind, will emerge to transfigure death and reorder the cycle of life.

Through the eyes of characters living on the fringe of industrialization, *Aje* grapples with the fear of death on one hand while cannibalizing natural resources on the other. In selfish pursuit, people are blinded to the natural order of the continuum and suffer the anguish of perceived endings. But when society dismisses the characters of *Aje*, their survival gradually restores and re-orders a continuum that only time challenges in the "end."

The name "Aje" comes from an ancient force described as being at once invisible and ubiquitous and whose history begins with existence. Although Aje predated the concept of "Yoruba," it is within this culture that the word signified the biological and spiritual power of African women who function as creators, sustainers, and destroyers of life. They are also known for extensively using natural resources such as herbs and animals for healing and empowerment.

CHARACTERS

NATANE 17-year-old, local Indigenous/Mexican American

BETTY 70s, local volunteer emcee for battle re-enactment

MAYOR MCCLOUD 60s, mayor of Aje, plays "Roman Nose"

RAMON 17-year-old, Latino, local athlete playing "Rookie Scout"

SHAWNA AND VICKI teenaged out-of-towners, spectators

ELBERT 40's, town jeweler playing an American Scout

INDIGENOUS BEATS Native American dance performance team from Denver

EXT. PRAIRIE GROUNDS - RE-ENACTMENT BATTLEFIELD - 1989 - DAY

SWING MUSIC cuts off. Gasps. A crowd aghast at a battlefield too real.

SIRENS from a sheriff cruiser and ambulance, bouncing over the rough brush.

The police cruiser dodges the goats who are finally coming to, and gets stuck, high-centered on the sandbar.

Ambulance EMTs run toward McCloud. Townsfolk huddle together, others wander off in shock.

A mini van pulls up with the circular logo of a Native American dancing framed by INDIGENOUS BEATS.

MEMBERS of the troupe slowly emerge from van dressed in their fancy dance regalia. The HEAD DANCER steps forward—

HEAD DANCER
What the hell's going on?

EXT. PRAIRIE GROUNDS TOP OF THE BLUFF - DAY

Elbert slides his headdress from head to heart.

Natane, on PONCHO the pony, rears to a stop several yards behind Elbert.

They share the same POV of dispersed confusion.

Natane emits an audible gulp.

EXT. PRAIRIE GROUNDS - BATTLEFIELD - DAY

Cody cuts through the crowd to Sheriff Meyer. He points to the bluff.

CODY
That's her, on Poncho! I saw it all!
She stole Mayor's pony!

Sheriff Meyer makes a beeline for the bluff.

EXT. PRAIRIE GROUNDS TOP OF THE BLUFF - DAY

Elbert spins to see Natane.

ELBERT
Natane! What are you—

NATANE
HEEEEYAW! Escape!

Natane and Poncho are off again.

ELBERT
HEY! Stop!

The sheriff, panting, scales the bluff.

ELBERT (CONT'D)
It's the Moreno girl, Sheriff!

They watch Natane disappear over the crest of a bluff.

EXT. TRAIN TRACKS/BRAWN'S DITCH - DAY

Ramon is walking with Shawna and Vicki flanking either side. He is lost in thought, chugging his beer. Shawna squints, incredulous.

POV Shawna: Natane speeding in the distance.

MINI MONTAGE: EXT. TRAIN TRACKS/BRAWN'S DITCH/DIRT ROAD - DAY Distant train.

Natane gallops parallel to train tracks. She sheds one piece of her dime-store costume at a time, the fringed gown, the headdress...

EXT. - DIRT ROAD - DAY

Distant train WHISTLE. Sheriff Meyer's police car speeds toward the oncoming train.

EXT. - BRAWN'S DITCH - DAY

Opposite side of the tracks. Ramon, Shawna and Vicki plop down a cooler in a deep barrel ditch. Shawna looks up and taps Vickie.

SHAWNA
Here it comes!

EXT. TRAIN CROSSING - DAY

Crossing guards DING and FLASH, lowering.

Sheriff guns it. The car swerves to an angled stop. The train guard clips the Thunderbird hood ornament.

EXT. - TRAIN TRACKS - DAY

Natane unfurls her braids, she looks back, the train is on her tail. Her long hair whips across her face.

EXT. - BRAWN'S DITCH - DAY

The teenagers press themselves against the ditch's walls. Pebbles clink, dust rains down.

EXT. RR TRACKS - DAY

Train WHISTLE. Throwing the gear shift into reverse, the police car shoots backward like a rocket.

SWOOOO—

EXT. - BRAWN'S DITCH - DAY

—OOOSSSH.

The train flies by. Shawna screams, laughing and grasping Ramon's hand. Vicki instinctively rolls into his arm for protection.

EXT. - ALONG TRACKS - DAY

Natane races the train, stripped down to shorts and T-shirt.

EXT. - BRAWN'S DITCH - DAY

In the privacy of deafening noise and flickering shadows, Shawna makes her move, then Vicki.

Ramon flinches then surrenders.

Natane's discarded headdress tangled up in a tumbleweed rolls over the make-out dogpile.

END OF MONTAGE.

EXT. PASTURE - SUNSET

A turn of reins, Natane veers away from the train and follows the meandering creek bed, hair flying.

The sky is a fiery orange.

EXT. FARMSTEAD - SUNSET

Natane dismounts mid-trot, on a slowing Poncho.

SQUAWKING chickens greet them. Natane quickly ducks into her house.

Poncho sniffs desperately at the creek bottom for water.

INT. KITCHEN - NATANE'S HOUSE - DUSK

Natane inches the table aside, turns a corner of the rug and squeezes through the hinged door.

NATANE (O.S.)
I'm coming!

INT. NATANE'S UNDERGROUND LAIR - DUSK

Natane descends earthen stairs.

She follows a dark corridor, a hand-held lantern illuminating an assortment of curios that look like a home-ec version of a Natural History display: animal trophies posed in fight or flight.

NATANE
(to self)
It's the ending. They never get it right.

She studies the collection like a taxidermist — tracing molars of a coyote jaw, inspecting the feathers on a bird, all while mimicking Betty, the MC of the battle re-enactment.

NATANE (CONT'D)
(to her trophy audience)
I tell you what, folks. There are a hundred tales of daring deeds, of self-sacrifice

She admires a buffalo skull upon an alter.

NATANE (CONT'D)
—of heroism unparalleled in an era when heroes were the rule and not the exception.

Natane puts a bundle wrapped in Jack's BBQ paper on her lap.

NATANE (CONT'D)
Thus concludes this tale — the greatest battle on the High Plains and you can quote Custer on that!

Natane starts unwrapping the bundle.

NATANE (CONT'D)
(mimicking Betty)
In honor of the Forsyth scouts- Alderice, Thomas. Armstrong, Walter. Bennett... Wallace, Boyle, Thomas. Burke...

She stops herself. She spreads the wrapper flat against her thighs to reveal a dead hawk.

NATANE (NO BETTY ACCENT) (CONT'D)
Mayor McCloud—

Her body trembles. She weeps silently. She looks up suddenly.

NATANE (CONT'D)
I'm in trouble.

EXT. ABANDONED FARMSTEAD - SUNSET

The Sheriff's car approaches.

INT. NATANE'S UNDERGROUND LAIR - DUSK

Natane spreads the hawk's severed wings and begins stitching with a strand of twine.

WUMP! We hear a car door slam from the outside world.

Natane freezes.

EXT. ABANDONED FARMSTEAD - SUNSET

Sheriff Meyer creeps towards the fence, a disheveled wreck.

The pony eats grass, reins still hanging.

SHERIFF MEYER
(patting the pony)
Hey buddy. Where's your rider?

He looks past the pony to the chicken shack and continues forward.

INT. NATANE'S KITCHEN - NIGHT

Natane peers out from the crack of the cellar door, listens.

The GATE outside SQUEAKS. CHICKENS CLUCK anxiously.

Natane quickly retreats.

INT. NATANE'S UNDERGROUND LAIR - DUSK

Water DRIPS melding into otherworldly SOUNDS: whispers, music, wind.

POV: Natane looks into the camera with reverence.

NATANE
The hawk can wait.

Natane exhales, shaking her hands in anticipation.

NATANE (CONT'D)
It's your turn. I didn't think my first time would be so important. I promise I'll do you right.

We now see who Natane has been talking to.

Her dead GRANDMOTHER is slumped on the ground, her eyes forward, her skin deceptively fresh and dressed for the day — found by Natane just that morning.

Natane slowly extends her hand to caress her grandmother's cheek. Natane draws her hand back suddenly. The touch of the cold flesh has snapped her back to reality.

RUSTLING SOUNDS above, SCOOTING furniture.

EXT. NATANE'S HOUSE - NIGHT

The sheriff straddles the kitchen door way, looking outside/inside.

SHERIFF MEYER (yelling)
Hey, kid.

Nothing.

SHERIFF MEYER (O.S.) (CONT'D)
Kid. Uh, Natane. Where are you?
What's going on?

INT. NATANE'S UNDERGROUND LAIR - NIGHT

Natane sprints from the room, zig-zagging in and out of shadows. She hits a wall, the end.

She looks up, face to face with a BABY, dead for 100 years, preserved perfectly like a 3D-tintype face.

Looking around, she is surrounded by generations of her

maternal ANCESTORS who resemble her in their preserved splendor.

She looks down to her feet. Water burbles up from the earthen ground.

EXT. NATANE'S HOUSE - NIGHT

Water comes up through the dried creek bed.

The sheriff, slips falling to his knees.

The pony cranes to drink the water.

The water continues to flow, more and more.

The sheriff dunks his face. He is overtaken - splashing, gulping, laughing. Water splashing, slurping, drenching himself.

Headlights approach. Gloria from the nearby farm house, steps out of her truck.

GLORIA
Sheriff Meyer? What's going on?

Suddenly the Sherrif grabs his throat. He's choking. The water is now sand.

Gloria's dog BRUNO runs over, BARKS uncontrollably.

GLORIA (CONT'D)
No, Bruno!

The dog growls at Gloria. She backs away but not before the dog lunges, snarling.

GLORIA (CONT'D)
Bruno! Bruno, stop!!!

A cacophony of pained screaming between Gloria and the sheriff.

The sheriff claws at his throat. He drops, rolls, covered in sand. Spitting, wiping grains from his eyes, his mouth.

INT. NATANE'S UNDERGROUND LAIR - NIGHT

The grandmother is lying near the edge of a pool of water in the ground. Natane kneels nearby. She paints a yellow line across her own forehead.

NATANE
Generation.

She traces her nose in red.

NATANE (CONT'D)
Birth.

Rubs black on her chin

NATANE (CONT'D)
Death.

She moves to her grandmother and lowers her into the

pool. The body floats and then slowly sinks, disappearing in one ripple.

Natane sees her own reflection.

NATANE (CONT'D)
Destiny.

animal encounters

Five Faunal Pieces Composed by Attendees of a Community Creative Writing Class Hosted by Anita Mumm

by anonymouses

Bobcat and Bunny

The bobcat was chasing a young bunny, equally as fast, but no doubt oozing fear. They disappeared for a sacred moment, then, suddenly, they were bounding by again, this time in the opposite direction.

I hug them back so they'll know I love them too, but I'm so tired. I've got to move on, I think, even though they want me to stay, but maybe I'll find "Mom" when I go. I'd like to give her another hug. I want to sleep in her lap, and just be held. This is good time to go to sleep, I think..

Cat

This sweet and moody cat, one of my mother's many furry companions, now with clouded eyes, unsteady on his paws. He's still eating, asking for every meal and every treat, and enjoying the food, but he's not thriving—his fur is matted and he's grown—no, shrunk—so skinny over the winter, with bones just under the skin, the once beautiful fluffy tail limp and drooping. He no longer smells like fresh air when he comes in the door, but he still asks to be picked up, he still nuzzles into my neck, just like he always did when mom held him.

Dogs

Late fall, early morning the dog walked me towards the usual path along the creek. Quiet soft air, a stillness greeted us. A creature twenty yards away caught my eye. My heart started beating in my throat. My mind fired up options if this stunning grayish brown coyote chose to attack my dog. The dog didn't bark. We were like three statues, no blinking eyes, thinking, staring. Seems we stood frozen for hours. She broke the stand-off and walked away.

Love this warm bumpy world
and this summer day. Here I am
surrounded by some beautiful flowers
& great crop of tomatoes - Golly is
that those - nasty grasshoppers - Do
I hear thunder or the opening of
a door & now it closes - thunder
shuffling - oh now the ~~woman~~ who
water plants - Boy is she ~~madder~~ was daughter -
How can I move faster who is nasty.
so she won't see me - useful.
Is this ~~my~~ the end inquires a
my wooly warm Vulture
Yes of well I be
transformed into a beautiful colorful
creature ~~to~~

Wooly Worm

There is a wooly worm, yellow with hair like fuzz, crawling up the stucco wall of my house, thinking; should I squash it? Will it make a nasty spot on my wall? Then I wonder; what will it become? Is it here to strip my plants, flowers, and veggies and have a feast? I wonder, will it sting me and cause an allergic reaction? Guess I will let it crawl a bit longer.

The dirt road was finally dry but still full of divets & rivets. I was tearing down the road, too fast, distracted by my husbands storytelling, when I saw a turtle in the dark underbelly of a tire canyon. We screamed. Crunch! Too late! Our hearts broke along with the turtle shell. Generally I keep my eyes peeled for turtles on the road because killing a turtle is about the biggest road kill sin of them all. Not this time. Alas

Turtle

The dirt road was finally dry but still full of divots and rivets. I was tearing down the road, fast, distracted by my husband's storytelling, when I saw a turtle in the dark canyon made by a truck's tire. We screamed, "Noooo!"

Crunch! Our hearts broke along with the turtle shell. Killing a turtle is the biggest road kill sin of them all.

A few days later, now on the highway, we saw another turtle. I braked, turned around, and drove back towards it. My husband jumped out and carried the turtle to safety, off the road in the direction it was traveling. It made me feel like less of a monster.

ditch driving

by Maureen Hearty

We were watching the sun set, cold cans of beer in hand. Meg, who was born and raised here on the plains of north-east Colorado, was telling me about a high school kid who'd recently driven too fast down an unlined two-lane highway, flipping her car into the ditch, and landing in the hospital. After so many similar stories had concluded with fatal consequences, the community was relieved that she'd survived with only a broken leg,

Ditches are those trenches alongside the road that channel off the water. Out here we've got dirt roads bounded by green ditches, which are just deep gutters full of grass and tumbleweeds, often at fairly steep slopes. Ostensibly, the ditches are about making you safer—until you accidentally steer into one during a rain storm. Or, worse, launch into while speeding home after a late night.

Did I mention that the roads are unpaved?

Meg, whose left arm was sunbaked into a crisp auburn from hanging out the window while driving her jalopy of a truck on a one hundred-and-fifty-mile rural mail route six days a week, had just finished telling me about the fugitive cow she'd hit the week prior.

The cow had totaled her pickup so she was borrowing her son's even shittier truck while fighting with the insurance company about who was responsible—her or the cow's owner. It's never the cow's owner.

I'd moved to the area one year ago after living in the city for most of my life. I didn't have a car in the city. I didn't need one; I had my bike and the bus. I'd like to say it was because I cared about pollution and my fitness, but it was because I didn't make enough money working at the homeless shelter to pay for a car, insurance, and gas. I also figured that by biking I was allowed to keep smoking because they cancelled out each other. Addict logic at its finest.

"It's only a matter of time" Meg continued, "before you end up in the ditch yourself. Cows, dust storms, muddy roads, blizzards, too many shots of Hot Damn. It's inevitable. And when it happens, you need to know what you're doing. Otherwise, you're gonna panic and find yourself flying out the window." She lit another Virginia Slim. "What I'm saying is: you need to practice your ditch driving." "

How does someone who has never driven into a ditch practice driving into a ditch?

Years passed with me never taking her advice. Until one summer night, driving my new-to-me manual pick-up home from a tequila session at the local motorcycle clubhouse, when my husband, Greg, announced that it was time.

"It's easy, just don't steer against the slope."

The tequila tempered my otherwise perfectly rational fear.

Greg continued. "Speed up a little bit but not too fast. You want to enter the ditch at a 30-degree angle. Scoop in and then scoop right out. Don't oversteer."

Perfectly simple. Shifting into fifth gear, I sped up. Common sense kicked in—for a moment—and I tapped the brakes. I shifted into neutral and slowly descended into the ditch and then, with a *whoop* I drove back onto the dirt road and skidded to a stop, the night air filled with dust.

"Not bad," said Greg. "Try it again, but faster."

This time, I picked up my speed and held it. I veered into the ditch at an altogether too-sharp angle, bottomed out, and killed the engine. The truck was perpendicular to the intended flow of traffic, rear wheels on the road, front wheels in the ditch grass.

"Shit," I said, defeatedly slamming my hands against the steering wheel

"Holy shit," said Greg. Directly before us, the pickup's headlights were shining on a burrowing owl who had perched on an old fence post.

"Holy shit," I repeated. Standing on the ground next to the fence post was a badger.

The owl and badger were looking directly at us. Then they looked at each other, longingly. Then back at us. They looked back at each other again, and their gazes seemed sad. Then the badger shrugged, clearly exasperated. I saw this. Then he broke the owl's gaze and waddled into the night like a grumpy flying-carpet.

The owl remained on the post, staring at us with a mix of shame and resentment.

"I don't think we were supposed to see that," I said.

I restarted the pick-up, and successfully shimmied back onto the road.

When we got home, Greg put on an old record by Al Green, and we toasted to the illicit romance of interspecies love.

Ten years have passed since that night. I've slid into plenty of ditches, but I've always kept my truck upright. Thanks, Meg.

everything is a cloud

by Nina Elder

In eastern Colorado, Denver is hidden by the western horizon. The same horizon obfuscates the magical machine that churns out daily thunderstorms. Every afternoon that I was in Joes, an accumulation of the invisible would come from the west, preceded by walls of wind.

I was transfixed. I made giant windsocks that attached to my head. I wrapped myself in white and stood with my feet in the green and my body in the blue.

I began seeing everything as clouds. My glass of water. My body. A conversation. Every. Thing.

An Incomplete Account of Things That Are Clouds

trees
cacti
bodies
rivers
oranges
the internet
closets
limestone
brains
magnets
valleys
sponges
drains
interstates
file cabinets
museums
archives
libraries
tree roots
gurus
churches
temples
black holes
vortexes
portals
intersections
stomachs
spring time
brainstorming
falling in love
deja vú
memories
dream worlds
hugs
land fills
trash cans
parking lots
thrift stores
wombs
government
zits
volcanoes
springs
factories
lungs
bombs
swimming pools
air ports
hearts
junctions
multiplication
berries
raffles
seeds
sinuses
boxes of kleenex
buffets
Semi trucks
School busses
mail boxes
voting
cities
bogs
schools
feed lots
siloes
cans
bottles
boxes
envelopes
sediment
cement
gas stations
note books
mysteries
families
gods
lakes
stampedes
mobs
ant hills
garages
traffic jams
elevators
trends
books
chapters
poems
sentences
religions
cultures
towels
forests
fields
lotion
septic tanks
sprinklers
bill boards
news papers
trains
herds
tribes
arguments
misunderstandings
wars
conflicts
romance
youth
health
pandemics
wind socks
anger
joy
sleeping
dreams
dancing
night clubs
feasts
meals
holidays
lines
distractions
grocery bags
pockets
suit cases
mountains
languages
equations
conversations
contracts
fields
expertise
curiosity
empathy
questions
agreements
pheromones
attraction
love
pianos
music
radio towers
sattelites
spies
songs
water balloons
time
myths
rumors
headlines
symbols
diamonds
words
charisma
seduction
sand dunes
pregnancies
aquifers

the iowa school for the blind

excerpted from the novel Rise of the Haugenberrys

by Zach Boddicker

A few hours of text and phone tag Tuesday and the trip to Bernfeld's was inked. We'd meet and leave from the Haugenberry house at 6AM Saturday and return whenever Sunday. This was sooner than expected, but there wasn't any reason to wait. We didn't have any prep work to do, Oliver had someone to cover the store, and Mr. Bernfeld was ready for us.

Everything went as planned Saturday morning, and we were on the east edge of the city by 6:30. The white tents of Denver International Airport to the north, the giant golf balls of Buckley Air Force Base to the south.

"Well, I'll be," Abe said, backhanding Dan on the thigh in an unexpected outburst of energy. We drove under the E470 overpass, at the frontier of Denver's urban sprawl. "We've got home field advantage again."

Dan shuffled through a stack of mail that had accumulated on the dash. Oliver and I were sitting not very comfortably in the back. Conversation had been sparse since we'd departed. Coffee hadn't quite kicked in, the sun was in everyone's eyes. We maintained some general silence, listening to NPR.

"Are you planning on using this?" Dan asked, holding a P.F. Chang's coupon mailer out for Abe to see.

"No," Abe said, annoyed by the interruption. "I don't even know where one is."

Dan tore the postcard-sized coupon in half, then quarters, then eighths. "Have you ever wondered what the P and F stand for?" he asked.

"No," Abe said. "Everybody knows already, and if you don't, who cares anyway?"

Abe started cycling through radio stations, eventually turning the radio off. I hoped we might start discussing a game plan for the recording.

"Everybody knows, huh?" Dan turned to consult Oliver and me. Neither of us could muster an answer.

"Peter Frampton," Abe said.

Dan started singing a Frampton song with the Ls and Rs jumbled up, like white dudes do when making fun of Asians who weren't raised speaking English.

Ooh baby I ruv your way, evley day

Frivolous, perhaps, but it was a tone-setter and icebreaker.

It got Oliver engaged, and the Frampton reference led to a conversation about groupie memoirs, the Ogallala aquifer, fracking, back to Frampton, and then a discussion between the brothers about alternative routes to Burg, and Bernfeld's place.

Abe exited at a town called Byers. The off-ramp took us over a dry river lined with dead cottonwood trees and decay of all sorts. Someone had set up shop at the crossroads ahead, selling right-wing flags and T-shirts from the back of his truck and camper. Abe turned to Oliver and me and asked if we wanted to stop and stretch a bit. It'd been an hour, and there wasn't ample room in the back seat, so it was time.

"What do you think, Dan. Should we go fuck with this guy?" Abe said, having already made up his mind, jerking the steering wheel to the left, skidding to a stop in front of the peddler's display, kicking up a thick cloud of dust.

Dan went for his door handle, and Abe stopped him. "New black truck, tinted windows. He probably thinks we're the feds. Try to look like a fed. Stone sober."

The dust cloud settled. The peddler was on his feet, cradling a lap dog, looking prepared to go for a firearm. Abe and Dan exited the truck, both in sunglasses, tucking in their shirts before approaching the peddler's tables. Oliver and I got out and stretched but kept close to the truck.

Good mornings were exchanged, and the peddler sat down on a lawn chair that the brothers eyed warily.

"Where you folks from?" the peddler asked.

Abe popped his knuckles before looking at the shrink-wrapped wares. "From Iowa, originally. Went to school there."

Dan grabbed the corner of the familiar yellow *Don't Tread on Me* flag that was hanging from a pole supporting the peddler's awning. He held it out and inspected it.

"Hawkeyes?" the peddler asked. "You must've been ball players."

Dan got Abe's attention. "This is one foolish-looking rattlesnake. I don't reckon you could come up with a dumber looking rattlesnake. Do you?"

Abe turned and looked for a moment, then turned his attention back to the spread of shrink-wrapped flags. "A *Far Side* reject."

"If I were a rattlesnake, and looked like this, I'd hope you'd stomp the shit out of me," Dan said, letting the flag drop. "Put me out of my misery."

"I'd be first in line," Abe said.

The peddler looked at Oliver and me for a moment, then back at Abe. "I'm gonna guess you two were on the Hawkeye basketball team."

No immediate response from either brother. Abe picked a book out of a box. I could see that he was holding it upside down.

"No," Abe said. "The Iowa School for the Blind."

Dan jumped in immediately. "Kay through twelve. You ever watch *Little House on The Prairie*? The TV show?"

"I remember it," the peddler said. "My kids watched it."

Dan turned to Abe. "You know who was a hot piece of ass on that show?"

"Merlin Olsen," Abe said.

"Mary—or whoever that actress was," Dan said. "The blinder she got, the hotter she got. All the fumbling around and blank looks. That's when she really came into her own as an objectified woman."

Abe explained to the peddler the connection between the TV show and the Iowa School for the Blind.

"Oh yes, I remember," the peddler said, petting his dog.

"Lots of crying on that show," Dan continued. "But they got one very important detail wrong."

The peddler's patience was nearing its limit.

"Blind people don't cry," Dan said. "That's how you knew for sure that actress wasn't blind in real life."

The peddler set his dog on the ground and stood, pulling a cigarette from a pack in his breast pocket. "You fellas don't look blind to me."

Both brothers stopped and stared at the man. Abe crossed his arms.

"We graduated, obviously," Abe said. "But it's intermittent. You have to keep on top of it."

"Top of our class, as a matter of fact," Dan said. "I'm gonna guess you're from China. All these flags and shirts—made in China. You're a long way from home!"

The peddler lit his cigarette. "One hundred percent American, born and bred."

Dan held out the *Don't Tread* flag again, inspecting the edges of it. "I'm trying to find the tag on this thing."

Abe picked up a Trump 2024 shirt, unfolded it, folded it backwards and placed it on the table. The peddler grabbed the shirt and began re-folding it. "Do you fellas plan on buying anything?"

Dan held out a corner of the flag, drawing attention to where a tag used to be. "Did you cut the tag off this?" he asked the peddler.

"Yes I did. So what?"

"If I buy this, how am I supposed to know how to wash it?" He pulled his Zippo from his back pocket and lit the corner of the flag.

"I hope you're planning on paying for that!" the peddler shouted. "If not, I'll gladly call the sheriff."

The flag burned quicker than Dan expected. He jerked it away from the pole and tossed it onto the ground away from everything else. It continued to burn, thick black smoke.

"There's no sheriff," Dan said.

Abe walked to the burning flag and began stomping on it. "Clapton shot him."

Dan tore another flag from the pole, lit it, and tossed it toward the other half-burnt flag. The peddler had his cell phone out, presumably to call the cops.

Abe looked at his wrist as though there were a watch wrapped around it. "Shit, Dan. We gotta be at P.F. Chang's in ten minutes."

Abe gestured for Oliver and me to get in the truck. Dan approached the peddler's table, removing his wallet from his jeans pocket. "Do you take cards?"

The peddler put his phone down. "You owe me twenty dollars."

Dan closed his wallet and put it back in his pocket. "I'll have to hit an ATM. We'll be back. You didn't tell us you were going to be here this morning. I'd have brought cash if you would've said something."

Abe drove over the still smoldering flag and onto the highway headed south. Oliver and I were still processing.

"Well, we've performed our civic duty for the day," Abe said. "I'm feeling better. Did you pay the man?"

"We paid him in memories."

the high winds blow

excerpted from the forthcoming novella It Will Follow the Rain

by Emmett Wilder

Forward

The High Plains is far from a retreat, and even further from a refuge. The wide-open expanse does little in the way of inspiring revelation or awe-striking the mind. At least, at first. Rather, the prospective artist must reconcile with the weight of loneliness and desolation.

If they pass this first trial, which is no easy feat, the artist is rewarded with a blank canvas. The weight lifts and the artist can begin to sketch, to paint, to bring word to paper, and finger to string. The land reveals itself as you discover yourself, and the nothingness falls flat as a false-front facade, and the persistent and curious discover a world brim with complex, beautifully interconnected life and millions of points of interest microcosmic to the prairie itself.

It is no coincidence that the first draft I've ever finished was begot whilst aimlessly exploring Yuma County. Faced with a land forgotten, I arrived expecting a daily program structured around artisanal blooming. I would've settled for a prompt. Instead, I was given an infinite leash and a tentative deadline: the death sentence for any artist. How can I create without intensive, bureaucratic pressure?

It turns out boredom is the surest fire way to reawaken a long-depressed sense of curiosity and wonder. Without the restraints of traditional programs with focused lenses of operation, my mind was encouraged to wonder, take risks, and create with the fullest sense of expression.

Colter Wall sings, "You got to fill the big empty, with little songs," and it is exactly this sentiment which I believe encapsulates Prairie Futures, and the undeniable power it wields not only in the ongoing environmental struggle unraveling our country, but also ourselves.

1

One day, a shadow fell over the western sky.

The heavens broke apart, ashen clouds surged forth,
descended over the mountains, and blotted out the sun.

A lonesome wind carried them past the foothills, across the
range, where they poured out their hearts until the streets
flooded and the yards turned to marsh.

When it was thru, the grass grew long, bent lazy in the
breeze, and the water went still, reflecting clear skies.

The cottonwoods shook out their snow, filled ditches,
caught in gutters, and bunched around telephone poles.
Children gathered piles and dove on them like autumn
leaves.

I stood on the back step admiring the geological oddity, and debated whether or not it was altogether worth drawing another breath.

•

In this story, I might have a name and if I did it would be something solemn.

I have witnessed the Earth and its revolutions time enough to know better and time enough to pretend I didn't.

I have known love to be a tightness in the chest and a levity in the mind and the only place I am content to be lost.

Find me a good man and I will wonder why I was born with a heart as contrite. Find me a bad man and I will wonder if it is worth it in the end.

•

Whether Hell might exist does not concern me.

I have found something close enough to it.

•

The air was crisp and my mouth fell open at the taste and just as soon came shut; my lips settled to a firm line, and lacking any meaningful reason to part them, I began walking.

2

I was born blindfolded on my knees.

When the high winds blew and shore the will from my hands, I held close to the ground and knew nothing else.

How endless, to wait.

How innate, the capacity.

To bide my time while nothing arrived.

When the blinds were lifted, it was with small hands and long eyes, and I knew then how something and nothing are all but the same, and my longing was thru.

3

Civilization collapsed like a dying star. A hundred thousand genealogies reduced to a speck on the horizon, hazy behind a pillar of smoke.

The sun let itself beyond the mountains, foothills pulled into their parent's shadow like a girl shy in the folds of her mother's dress.

When the moon cast the prairie aglow, I watched the last barren peak, swallowed up by a modest mound of earth.

My boots wore thin.

My soles ached, sloughed away, calloused over.

Stitches gouged my sides and stifled my breath.

My lips grew so parched, if I'd had any reason to split them, they would have crumbled to dust, whisked with the wind.

I stood in ditches, soaked in puddles.

My mind ambled along, freed from the burden of existence. Lying easy in cerebrospinal fluid as one lies in the Dead Sea, so thick with salt you might stare up at the stars and fall into the sky.

Time stretched out its wings, suspended in flight.

The plains unfurled an easy lope.

Past sun-bleached barns and derelict homes. Sagging power lines and diving birds. Families of bison so far and few between, one could hardly believe they once coated the land in a shroud so vast the prairie was swallowed whole like the night.

Towns remembered and towns forgotten. Names spat and names sung.

Along the verge or clustered against foundations, shrines to a dead religion: rotting tires, rusting rotary tillers, appliances stripped for parts.

A mannequin toppled across the road, staring blankly at the sun.

Left behind in the desert to clutch a hole in its chest.

The few differences in elevation put one another aside to contend with the dilapidated buildings squatting amongst them, and upon passing a name neither spat nor sung, I collapsed in the dust and knew my wandering had come to end.

4

How infinitely rare, the quality of compassion.

To lay still and listen, with the warmth of touch and the shape of timbre.

The fragility of it.

It is no easy thing, to love a man. Harder even, to love this one.

She was altogether rare.

•

Held between two hands.

Tenderness assumed with a wounded animal lost in the dark, and that's what I was, what she was. What I am.

•

To grow together, to grow old together.

To surrender some, that the sacrifice is sweeter; a butterfly shedding its chrysalis, and that infinitesimal moment, wriggling free from its carapace and unfurling its wings, feeling for the first time the lightness of air and freedom of space, to lift up and embark a life its pupal self could never have imagined.

If anything I have done beneath this sun was ever worth its salt, it would be because of her, of that I have no doubt.

5

Sand beneath my knees.

I fall to my side, let it cool my skin and the hair on my brow, turn black with sweat, with acceptance of this, of death.

An emerald eye over a shoulder. Golden locks wet with spray. A bottom lip, full and curved. Wavelets lapping the shore.

Hold it there. Fill that space in my chest until it's overflown.

Until my eyes close like the rising moon and the falling night and if that coldness comes, I should not feel it.

•

Something sharp, a peck across the lips.

Blink bleary.

Beady black eyes stare down from a half-cocked head.

Peel yourself from the asphalt.

Watch the crow bob its beak and flit its feathers, up, over.

Far away.

6

Abandoned buildings hunch weary at the road.

Collapsed and crumbling, windows shuttered and chimneys felled. Thickets grown over dry.

I stagger down the road, shards of stained glass crunching underfoot.

An oxidized cross hangs limp from weatherworn vinyl. Across the street, a corroded letter *D* sinks in the sand before a shack overgrown in withered ivy.

Provided the choice between two vices, I opt for the one responsible for destroying fewer lives.

Inside, the air is thick. Dead leaves shrivel and rot, litter the linoleum. Grimy brown-bottled beer and dusty liquors. I rub my thumb across a whiskey sleeve and it comes away black.

A few tepid bottles of water in the shadow of a cooler. I pull the door back, it catches on the track, skips the groove, and clatter to the floor.

On my way out, I slip the whiskey in my jacket.

The sun sinks in the bare-blue blanket of the sky.

Wind yet to blow.

Fractured eyes stare up from the crimson mosaic, long and harrowed. The heat shimmers low over the pavement, turns them watery. The shards draw lines across my face, and I am old.

I run my hand along my jaw.

A bead of water trickles over the tarmac.

I blink.

A few more, coursing thru the glass.

I wet my fingertips.

The ground shudders.

Turn from the reflection.

A monstrous wave rears over the prairie.

Holds still, spume spilling from the peak.

Face swelling, hungry.

Mist over the maw.

A figure, lost beneath the goliath, looks over a shoulder.

I close my eyes.

All the sound in the world, one colossal sigh collapsing on the shore.

•

A horn, blaring.

Headlights.

Stare, slack-jawed.

Scramble back.

The tanker roars by, a speck in the wind.

Clamber to your feet, steady your breath, the air in your lungs.

See an old man's face gaze back a thousand times, marooned and haggard.

Says, What *are* you doing?

GUNSHOP

the goal is to delight yourself

Eleven Prosodic Pieces Composed at a Community Writing Workshop Helmed by Claire Boyles

by anonymouses

Sleep

How complicated can it be? You lay down, close your eyes, shut your mind off...Oh, that's the kicker! Shutting your mind off. Is it a decision that you make and, voila—sleep? Or is it magic? You say a magical word—your mind goes blank and la la land comes and all worrying ceases and blissful rest overtakes you.

It shouldn't be this hard. Everybody does it (don't they?) Why not me? Is there something wrong with me? Looking for just a little bit of normal.

Wonder

I wonder why I am here
Why are you here

How a teacher can teach non-writers
Why other people aren't here
What was that bird trying to say
Why god made flies

If it will rain this weekend
And how much snow will fall this winter
And when will I go to Indiana

When will Misery learn to not climb on kitchen
    counters

The Great Past Time

Puzzling over thoughts.
Sometimes it might be more like day dreaming.
Some might even say it's a waste of time.

All kinds of things come from wonder—art—
magnificent paintings or whimsical drawings.
Music, from Mary Had a Little Lamb to
Beethoven's Ninth?

What happens if I mix these solutions?
Medical marvels.

I wonder therefore I am.
Wonder on and on
Astrologers
Explorers
Planet Earth

I wonder why I can't sleep.
Maybe it is so I can wonder wonder wonder
Thinking of all the wonderful wonder all around.
Thankful I can wonder too.

Worry

I know the general outline of worry / panic...it is the emotion that haunts my nights...it keeps me awake at night...it sometimes rules over me, bidding me to obey...it is faceless but terrifying...there is no rhyme or reason...no time...no season.

It is a cruel taskmaster sapping my strength and my energy. I live like a zombie, a night creature who roams the darkness finding no peace. The days bring sleep but no rest.

The purpose is gone.

Do something

It isn't

There's no place. So much to

start

Rude

Gee, you look terrible today.

Well I tried my best to look presentable but I only have some much to work with.

We will move on from here.

Inherited

From the other side of it, if my sibling got it I would feel the grudge.

Deal with the grudge.

Trash can the grudge.

Dire warning

"Yes, and about the lack of entertainment in the afterlife..."

Dog on road

Along the lonesome Highway 36, something darts out of the corn.
A beat-up scotty dog.

She brakes.

The semi full of corn nearly rear-ends her. The driver gives her the finger as he speeds past.

She grabs the bag of jerky, slams the car door and makes her way to the dog.

The dog, covered in sandburs and dreadlocks, isn't interested in the jerky.
The dog is interested in her; her crouched posture and open hands.
Face lick.

She makes room in the passenger seat.

THE ECKLEY GARAGE

Conversation between child and parent concerning the topic of sex

Ask your mom.

Kitchen

I find it hard to be in her kitchen.
It's not the size, an alleyway kitchen with limited
counter space and no windows.
It's the mess.
Wednesday's spaghetti sauce hardening on the side
of a cracked bowl.
Soft brown bananas next to crumbled cheese.
No clean cups and it's hard to wash one in the
avocado green sink full of her son's nacho
party dishes.

I'd grab a soda from the fridge but I'm afraid to
open it.

"Can we go sit outside and enjoy the fresh air?"

Unfortunate

I inherited a work of art that my sister coveted and always believed would be hers. She'll believe that I robbed her again. She'll imply that I'm always the lucky one, the favorite. Little does she know it will be hers by year's end. Grandma knew my diagnosis wasn't favorable. My fortunate, spoiled, little sister.

three poems

by Andrea Moore

Sunday

It's Debora's birthday
And Sarah's birthday
It's a Sunday in November.
There's a war on.
It snowed today in Tesuque,
And in La Villita a slate sky froze the world
In stillness.

In a tiny scratch
On the top of the hand-hewn wooden table,
There is a sesame seed
Stuck so snug in the scratch
I hardly saw it at all.
We did our Arabic homework
Together at that table

Conjugating verbs

Learning to write legibly
In this new alphabet.

On the phone,
Melanie asked about my progress
With textile art and natural dyeing
The way we'd all prefer to dye
And I explained I'd lost some confidence,
But I was writing every day.
She said not to worry –
This is how it goes sometimes,
And something new would arise.
She said the Ozempic makes her feel
Nauseated at night
From her intentionally empty stomach –
She's starving
Starving –
And it seemed I might feel permanently sad.

There's no relief.
Even when there's no war on,
There's a war on.

Ice Cream

The truck is white.
The girl in the advertisement
On the side of the truck
Is white.
She is happily licking an ice cream cone –
Vanilla.

The people surrounding the truck
Are brown.
They are crowding, surging.
They surge and strain to see
Inside the ice cream truck.
Icy condensation billows
From the truck's open door.

The phone camera held high
Sees where humans can't.
It reaches past their shoulders
And over their heads.
It can see inside the ice cream truck,
Can see the bodies in the ice cream truck.
The bodies in the ice cream truck
Are wrapped in
White sheets,
Stained red.

The long bodies are stacked on top of each other,
The names of the dead scrawled in black script
Across their grim wrappers.

The crowd surges.
The keeper of the dead –
The ice cream man? –
Is out of his depth.

Flaming Gorge: A Recreation Area

Flaming Gorge is shaped like a bleed,
A seep,
A spill, a lick of fire,
A many-fingered flare.
The reservoir of water is fashioned
Like a fracture, like a quake;
It's shaped like a mistake.
There used to be a river,
And then they built a dam.
The dam backed up the water,
'Til the river was a lake.
The valley gulped, but it went under,
And now the landscape is an ache.
It's green,
And blue,
But kind of fake.

For me, the jet skis take the cake.

Before the flood,
They cleared the crowd.
Well, the settled few
The one, or two, or ten,
Or more who'd built small houses
Not on a lakeshore,
But in a mountain glade.
See the fingered lake.

Remember, back before,
Down below, was
Land. Not just sand, but
Trees and rocks and scrub and sage
The bones of human ancestors
The memory of Ms. Minnie's rage.

Ms. Minnie, she had moxie.
When they cleared the valley,
Her house was slated to submerge.
She had the men from town to tea.
They sat down hopeful,
Pitched their proposal:
Assistance moving,
Money down.
Minnie smiled with her mouth,
But her forehead furrowed in a frown.
Who the fuck do you think I am?
(Cups and saucers,
Stacks of papers)
You think I built this dream to drown?
She didn't sign.
She burned it down.

Where Minnie went next, God only knows.
But swimming, the tingle in my toes
Knows below Ms. Minnie flows.
Shame on you
Her finger wags.
Like a wraith,
A watery, waving
Strand of grass,
Clasping at ankles,
Shudder to think.
I kick at the cold,
Reflect and refract.

There were rabbits in this valley
Rodents, snakes, and deer
Foxes, surely, bears, and more –
I saw a bluebird just before.
Did they all scramble two by two
Up the hillside as the water rose?
No ark, no, but a
Motorboat cuts a stripe across the sky.
I see it there –
Above that tree.
I am sitting on a stone

While a lake is sitting here on me.
All the burrows are submerged
All the foxes shifted shape
And now are fish
And all the fox and fishes' wishes
Rush like bubbles to the surface
And burst against my skin,
While I tread water in the lake
That never should have been.
The water's glass, and looking down
I see me writing on the ground.
And looking up, I see me too
And two by two I'll try to flee
The flood that has encompassed me
For I am not a unicorn
I am not a binary.
I will swim, *and* I will sink.
When they build a reservoir,
Even as I drown,
I'll drink.

PAINT
$5.00
PER GALLON

successful artistry in three parts

More Lessons in Failure

by Gregory Hill

PART I

I enter the air-conditioned lobby with a wooden milk crate full of books balanced on my shoulder. Enthusiastic signage confirms that I've found the Englewood Library Author Fest, where I shall participate in this afternoon's author panel on Publishing in Colorado.

Arranged within the perimeter of the lobby are merch tables laden with stacks of books. Sitting behind the tables are the books' respective authors. It's almost lunchtime. These writers have been here since 9:30 and the vibe is weary.

This is the Author Showcase segment of the Englewood Library Author Fest. Engage with the public, sell some books, practice your elevator pitch. I've opted to skip this part; I do not know how to talk strangers into reading my novels.

The books in the crate on my shoulder will be given away to the various like-minded authors I intend to meet today.

. . .

Ah, here's an author I intend to meet. His name is Dudley. I recognize him from the emails. Dudley has a handsome stack of books on his table. I recognize him from his profile photo on the Author Fest webpage. He wrote a book about the history of Englewood. He'll be with me on the panel this afternoon. I approach in a manner that I hope will be interpreted as jocular.

"Say," I say, "I just drove in from the Eastern Plains and I wonder if you could help me out. I'm a little disoriented on account of I haven't seen another human in several weeks."

I shift the milk crate off my shoulder and rest it upon the table. I tip it so he can see that it contains books. I say, "My name's Greg. I think we're on a panel after lunch."

He grips the table with both hands and twists his torso to look behind himself. I think I've frightened the old fellow.

I say, "You're Dudley, right?"

He untwists himself. "Uh-huh," he says.

"I think we're on a panel together. At 1:45. Publishing in Colorado, or something."

Dudley says, "Don't know anything about that."

He watches closely as I pick up a copy of his book and read the back cover.

> *Did you know that something exciting happened in Englewood, Colorado in the year 1858 that changed the course of American History?*
>
> *Want to know more, then, this book is for you!*

"Twenty dollars," says Dudley.

I return the book to the stack and back away.

Say, is that Blaine over yonder? Blaine's on the panel, too! I haul my crate to his table.

"Hi. Blaine, right?"

"Sorry?"

"Yes, I'm Greg and—"

"Speak up."

"—it's good to meet you. I'm on the panel after lunch."

"I don't think I know you."

"I don't imagine you would, seeing as we've never met. Until now. Ha, ha."

Blaine tilts his head. "So we have established that we don't know each other."

"Uh," I say.

Blaine redirects his attention to a hangnail.

In an attempt to know Blaine a little better, I direct my attention to the back of his book.

One moment you might cringe reading about billions of locusts descending on farmland. The next you may laugh out loud at anecdotes and original poetry.

Wait, Blaine's with Outskirts Press? Four queries and they couldn't even bother to send me a rejection.

I return the book to its stack and move on.

I've come to the Englewood Library Author Fest in an attempt to escape the malaise that followed the release of my fourth novel. You ever see one of those nature documentaries where they rescue an injured wolverine and then, when it's feeling better, they bring it back to nature and they open the door to its cage and the critter instantly waddles into the woods and everybody gets all teary eyed and proud?

My fourth novel refused to leave the cage.

My mantra for the day is *Don't let the bitterness show.*

. . .

Lookee, it's Colleen, a novelist and the fourth member of the panel. Her table is wedged between those of a romance writer and a historical-romance writer. She's currently engaged in a conversation with the historical-romance writer. I catch a fragment.

"...it be so cool if an agent just showed up..."

I take this moment to scan Colleen's back cover.

> *This compelling and exciting fictional story depicts the lifelong journey of a mother and daughter struggling to remove themselves from the restrictive tentacles of life in a small town dominated by a conservative, misogynistic religion.*

That's right in line with my fourth novel. We're peers!

Colleen turns away from the historical-romancer and says to me, "Hi there! My book is a compelling and exciting fictional story that—"

"I'm Greg. Tickled to meet you."

"—depicts the lifelong journey of a mother and daughter struggling—"

"I think we're on the panel together. After lunch."

"—to remove themselves from the restrictive tentacles—"

I say, "Funnily enough, I, too, wrote a book about..." I extract from my crate a copy of Novel #4. "...a group of women who—"

"—small town dominated by a conservative—"

I think I might be a ghost.

A bell dingalings. A library volunteer announces, "Luncheon is served."

"Good to know you," I say to Colleen. "Perhaps we can discuss this deeper at—"

"—misogynistic religion."

I leave my book on Colleen's table and carry my crate to the men's room where I repeat my mantra into the mirror several times.

. . .

The caterers give me a bag containing a salad, chips, and a brownie. I fill a plastic cup with lemonade.

I scan the hall for an appropriate dining partner. There are several circular tables scattered about. Colleen has not yet arrived. Nor have Dudley or Blaine. At each table is seated exactly one author. I choose the most autistic-looking of the lot—under the assumption that I, a spectral being myself, might successfully relate to him.

Out of respect for our respective conditions, I leave two seats between us. He barely moves his cube-shaped head as I sit.

I say, "How was your morning?"

"Not bad."

"I presume you write books."

"I do, but today I'm just staff."

Underneath his flannel is a baby-blue T-shirt reading *Book Festival Staff.* I quick look around. Baby blue everywhere. Shit, half the people here are on staff.

I ask him if he knows where to go for the author panels.

He says, "I do. In fact, I'm facilitating one. Publishing in Colorado. Greg, right? I'm Clayton."

Delightful. "What do you write, Clayton? When you're not on staff?" I'm actualizing my secondary mantra, *Exchange your mouth for your ears.*

"Philosophy."

I should see if I can get him to teach me something. I say, "Who's your go-to?"

"I've written four books about Nietzsche."

"Uh, tell me—" Shit. I've started a question without knowing what the question will be. I do this when I'm trying to show off to strangers, especially strangers who've written four books about Nietzsche. And now I've got about half-a-second before this gets—ah, I've got it.

"Tell me, Clayton, could you compare and contrast the ways in which 'God is dead' has been misinterpreted with the ways that 'We're more popular than Jesus' has been misinterpreted?"

He does not immediately reply. My syntax was confusing. He might be too young for the Beatles reference.

"Interesting. A very *American* construct."

I picked the right table.

"You guys talkin' about jelly?"

Fuck. It's Dudley. He sits equidistant from me and Clayton. We're each of us separated by 120 degrees.

"Nietzsche," I say, "and the Beatles."

"Blaine should be here," says Dudley. "He wrote a whole book on bugs."

"The mop tops," I say. "The Beatles. Ed Sullivan. *Yeah, yeah, yeah.*"

"I prefer jam, myself."

I look to Clayton for a sympathetic wink. Right, brother? Nope. He is pressing his phone against his face.

Change of tack. Let's find out what lurks inside Dudley's noggin. "Come," I say to the man who doesn't recognize me from six minutes ago. "Sit closer so that we may visit."

Dudley sits next to me. And off he goes. "If the government tells me I can't take water out of the river in my backyard, then I shall tell the government—pardon the expression—FUCK YOU."

It's not Nietzsche, but who knows.

I say, "Water rights are complicated." I could elaborate, but I can't.

"Water rights are simple," huffs Dudley. "Kansas and Oklahoma think they own it all."

"*Don't tread on me*, eh?"

"Hangin' on my flagpole."

One of *those* critters. The thing about Dudley's particular species is that there's only one of them. Different bodies, sure, but their brains all run on the same operating system. Outdated, slow, and riddled with viruses. You'll never get an original thought out of a Dudley. They're like talking bumper stickers.

Before Dudley can elaborate on his flagpole, we are interrupted by an announcement from Miranda, whose name I recognize from various emails. Miranda has facilitated this event. A fully-functional human, she speaks clearly, welcomes the authors, thanks the sponsors, thanks the caterers. Encourages us to mingle.

Miranda concludes with, "And, so, we now have to do something called a Land Acknowledgement. Ahem. *The land underneath this library was originally home to the Cheyenne and the Arapahoe—"*

Dudley's arthritic fingers tear open his bag of spicy jalapeño chips. A cloud of crumbs spills onto the table. He says to me, bristling, "You know who gets a bad rap. George Armstrong Custer."

"Please continue," I say. Perhaps he's a different kind of Dudley. My tertiary mantra is *Avoid confrontation.*

"All them people, they call him a monster. But the morning of the Last Stand, Custer explicitly told his men not to shoot any non-combatants. Don't shoot the women and children, he said."

I say, "What about the men?"

"Exactly. One of Custer's men lifted his rifle and said, 'I'll shoot anyone I please!' And so Custer rode up to him with his sword and said, 'Lower your weapon.' And he did. See? People don't want to remember that part."

"I see. And how'd that work out for everybody?"

Dudley makes a sound like a slowing locomotive. "He did his best, given the circumstances."

"So," I say, "you're telling me Custer wasn't *entirely* a sack of shit?" Oops. I've just violated at least two of my mantras.

"You know your problem," says Dudley, recognizing me from a million cable news nightmares, "is that you've got too many micro aggressions."

Clayton is now muttering nonsense words into his telephone.

I say, "Anything else you'd like to tell me about myself?" I've turned salty. Because I don't appreciate the way Dudleys are always reducing people to cartoonish stereotypes. I know. Lest ye be, and all that.

"It's the original texts that matter," says Dudley. "Not this 'new history'. Newspapers of the time. That's the truth."

Any minute, he'll start in on how no one cares about our heritage anymore, which will segue directly into a condemnation of the lack of respect for innocent statues.

I say, "Newspapers written by who?" Wait, should it be *whom*? If it follows a preposition—oh, shut up, brain. My mantras are all mixed up. *Don't let the confrontation show the mouth the bitterness.*

Dudley says, "Written by people of the time. Before everybody started microing everything."

"Right. And who were these people?" It has become imperative that I get Dudley to acknowledge that his beloved newspapers were written by sensationalistic white folk.

Clayton is now rubbing his phone against his forehead, as if it were an ice cube on a hot day. With his spare hand, he gathers his disposable dinnerware and exits.

"The truth," says Dudley, "is obvious."

I unwrap my brownie from its cling wrap. Without thinking, I offer it to Dudley. Apparently, my subconscious is trying to keep this from getting out of hand. Good work, brain.

Dudley politely declines the brownie. Maybe my mantras *are* working.

I'm going at this wrong. I need to try something less micro. I say, "Do you come across a lot of Indian newspapers in your research?"

"You bet. There's one called *The Painted Horse* or something or other. But that's only in the last twenty years or so."

"And therefore it can't be accurate, at least with respect to historical events."

"You're gettin' it now." Dudley is proud of me.

A bell dingalings. Lunch is over.

A high-school volunteer leads me to the lecture room. She has braces. I tell her I'm losing my mind. She tells me it's okay. I ask her if she reads books. She does. I give her a copy of Novel #4.

Blaine and Dudley and Colleen are already there, sitting at the table behind placards with their names and author photos. My placard is at the far end of the table, next to Colleen's. Mine is the only photo that includes barbells.

Opposite the table are two rows of plastic chairs. The chairs outnumber the audience three-to-one. No one is sitting in the front row. We've still got a couple of minutes—Clayton has not yet arrived—so I move all of the front row chairs behind the second row.

I say, "It's more intimate this way." Mild amusement.

I slide into my seat next to Colleen.

A fifth spectator enters. He marches directly to the new back row. This elicits mild smiles from those of us who are in on the joke.

Clayton arrives, carrying a barstool, and plops it down next to me and sits upon it. He introduces the authors by way of reading our bios, then he looks at the clock, which shows 1:42. "Let's give it another minute. In case of late-comers."

He kills time with a few words about himself, starting with Nietzsche and quickly evolving into a series of increasingly strident complaints about philosophy students and laptop computers. This is a man who could use some mantras.

The second-hand swings to top-dead center on 1:45 and Dudley cuts off Clayton with a wheezy, "The problem is, everybody thinks everybody's gotta be a damned winner."

Clayton calls the panel to order.

. . .

Forty-five minutes later, the panel concludes.

Full statistics:

Clayton: Two minutes of speaking time spent asking sixteen variations on "Where do you get your ideas?"

Blaine: Twelve minutes of speaking time. Nine of which concern his grandchildren.

Colleen: Seven minutes of speaking time. We learn that she's a tennis pro and that her son died during Covid, in a bike accident. Writing her novel helped her get thru the grief. I make a note to think nicer things about her.

Me: Less than one minute. Witty and brief with minimal cynicism. Not bad, considering.

Dudley speaks for forty-five minutes. We learn that the snow plow was invented in Englewood.

Number of times publishing is mentioned: Zero.

The high school volunteer returns to usher me out of the library. As we approach the exit, Miranda the Organizer hustles forth.

"Greg! Finally! I've been meaning to thank you. For your email."

"You're most welcome. What email?"

"We were having a rough day last week. Rough week, actually." Her expression goes dark. "This has been way more complicated than we anticipated." She smiles. "But you made us laugh."

"Aw."

"Seriously."

I don't remember the email, exactly, but I remember, now, why I sent it, and why I'm here, and why the four-hour round-trip for a free lunch with Dudley and forty-five minutes of not talking about publishing has been worth it.

I say, "I wish to speak sincerely."

Miranda nods permission.

"Writing can be lonely and depressing and it can make you feel like you don't exist. We're a needy bunch, authors, and largely delusional. This festival has given all of us permission to believe in our delusions for a day. The way you put this together, you've treated all of us as if we were professionals. In my experience, this does not happen to writers, ever. Except this time. I am grateful to you."

"Aw," she says.

I'm inspired, and so I continue when perhaps I shouldn't. "For the first time in years, the thought of writing doesn't make me feel even the tiniest bit like killing myself."

Miranda hugs me, skillfully avoiding the box that I'm clutching against my belly. I don't like being hugged. But this one was okay.

"Drive safe," she says.

PART II

It's mid-afternoon. I have to be back in Joes in two hours, for I am to be the sound guy for the musical act at this evening's Prairie Futures Market. Prairie Futures gigs are technically simple. Point some microphones at the singers. Point some speakers at the audience. Beg the band to play as quietly as possible.

Simple or not, it doesn't matter; my autismal tendencies inflate every sound guy job into a goddamned Hindenburg. Somehow, everyone else seems to deal just fine.

The Prairie Futures Markets take place on an acre of vacant land at the west end of our vacant town. The site is pretty, with well-kept gardens of native grasses and flowers and a generally chill vibe. In the middle of the site is a post-modern concrete sculpture/picnic area. The local community tends to view this—the sculpture, the Market, the whole thing—with unbridled wariness.

Maintaining Prairie Futures requires a ton of work. I know this because my wife, Maureen, does a great deal of this work. She writes grants, pulls weeds, pays local kids for half-assed garden maintenance, patiently endures the Port-a-Potty guy's wackadoo conspiracies. Hires the soundman.

As I'm exiting the Denver-metro area, the radio announces the imminent arrival of a vicious thunderstorm to the High Plains of eastern Colorado. Torrential rain, potential tornadoes. Hail, they predict, will reach the size of a fifty-cent piece, a coin that has not been in circulation since well before I wore pants with pockets.

My rearview mirror is filled with dark clouds.

An hour later, halfway home, the fifty-cent-piece clouds have grown into battleships, darkening the sky to the northwest. They are keeping pace with me, catching up, even.

I reach the Prairie Futures site simultaneous to the first timid sprinkles of rain. The site is set back from the highway, behind a farmhouse whose lower level is occupied by Barb, a pleasant woman of a certain age, always eager to meet the latest oddball artists Maureen has lured for their week-long residencies in the cozy apartment upstairs.

There's a small huddle of humans at the food truck, awaiting their orders. I am famished, ready to claim my agreed-upon sound-guy salary of one smothered carne asada burrito, no queso, no crema. As I approach the truck, a human informs me that they're not taking any more orders, followed by a glance at the sky, as if there's any question why.

The food-truckers hastily toss four Styrofoam boxes to four sets of hands. Moments later, the truck is accelerating due east on Highway 36.

I can't wait to tell Maureen about my day. There she is, and why is she hauling a PA speaker up the steps to the artists' apartment?

Maureen is careful to explain to visiting artists that a Prairie Futures gig will be considerably different from what they may be used to. Under *ideal* circumstances, the audience—that is, the portion of the market-goers who are actively paying attention to the performance—will be mostly elderly and sober and eager for any morsel of live music. It's a demographic gumbo that one rarely encounters, say, in a dive bar.

Children with flowers behind their ears will chase one another across the stage. Certain toddlers have discovered the thrill of twisting amplifier knobs mid-performance. At some point, someone's going to approach the lead singer mid-lyric and ask, "You ever hear of a song called Wagon Wheel?" A cheerful farm dog will arrive and seek affection from those who are not afraid of its clotted fur. One night, a white horse with a bad ankle limped past the stage and then disappeared into the dark. Ask Teague. He was there.

Remarkably, there have never been any issues with any of this. It certainly helps that the musicians actually get paid. Not a fortune, but enough to cover the gas and still clear high double digits for each musician, which is somehow better than a typical Denver gig.

I intercept Maureen as she's coming down the stairs to retrieve another portion of the PA system. It is unwise to begin a conversation by second-guessing. This is exactly what I do.

"You're really going on with this? They say it' going to hail." The rain continues its gentle sprinkle.

Maureen marches past me, heads toward her pickup. I should have led with *I love you, darling, how can I help*?

My idiocy proceeds apace. "I've been watching the storm since I left Denver. It's demonic."

"I hadn't noticed." I detect sarcasm. "I'm kinda busy, if you can believe it. The woman who was supposed to deliver the lecture on sustainable farming canceled. There's hardly anyone here. The band has locked themselves in their RV. The clouds are about to explode. We no longer have a food truck. And I've got seven people asking me what to do."

The work that she puts into these things. Hours of meetings, negotiations with presenters, finding a food truck, and driving herself mad trying to locate a microscopic Venn overlap that might allow her to introduce some environmental awareness to a farming community that's sucking dry the very underground water source that, for the past sixty years, has sustained the entire agri-infrastructure that fuels the region's star-spangled self-esteem.

Maureen surrenders neither to storms nor skeptics. That's why she's been able to sustain her community projects in Joes for the past ten years in spite of the overwhelming indifference of the community. It's also how she's managed to sustain a relationship with me for the past twenty-five years.

I say, "Can I talk to the band? Maybe they—"

"As I mentioned, they're in the RV."

"And they're aware of the weather?"

"If you don't want to be here, you can go."

She's off to improvise an answer to the next uncertain actor.

In the distance, lightning has begun snapping between the clouds and earth. Months of preparation are crumbling.

Asa, the Boulder grad student approaches me. We met a few months ago, a good chat over a good meal. Asa is from Vermont. He has never seen a storm like this, and so I cannot resist. In spite of my attempts to grow up, there remains within me a toxic relic of my youth that compels me to fuck with city slickers.

"That," I say to Asa, with a nod to the expanding cumulonimbi, "is an Eastern Colorado Thunderfucker."

I alert him to the imminent arrival of fifty-cent-piece hail. Asa, who is my junior by multiple decades, has probably never seen a fifty-cent piece. To illustrate, I make the OK sign. "About that big. It's not the mass you have to worry about, it's the fact that they're flat, like a coin, and they come down so fast they'll slice right thru the roof of your car."

"You're kidding."

"There was this one time—Wowzer! You see those white streaks? There, just above the horizon. That's hail." Or not.

Wind pushes against us. Asa shudders. "Did you feel that?"

"That'd be the cold front. Shit's about to get serious."

"Oh man. I'm leasing my car."

"Gimme a minute."

Maureen is with one of her seven charges, discussing desserts. I interrupt. "You mind if I lead Asa to the farm? We'll park his car under a roof and come right back."

"Fine. Go."

"Follow me," I say to Asa. The first proper raindrops have launched.

I drive, he follows in his car. Two miles of highway, then a left turn followed by two miles of dirt, buffeted by wind, field-dust, and slashing rain, then we turn into the farm and I direct him toward the shed and I open the big door and we drive our cars inside. As the big door slides closed, the torrent begins in earnest. The rain is violent and the shed is sheet metal, and so it is thunderously loud. Until the storm passes, this is where we are.

Asa and I are wearing ear mufflers, the kind that yellow-lens gunsters don at the firing range. To kill time, we play a round of H-

O-R-S-E. There's a basketball hoop in the shed. Asa is taller than me. He's not a basketball player, he claims. I am, I claim. Asa destroys me. He's very polite about the drubbing, even though he has to shout to be heard.

I crack open the hanger doors, lee of the storm so rain won't blow in. Waves of wet wind set the prairie grass to flail. A drive-thru carwash comes to mind.

Asa marvels. "It's like a hurricane."

I'm pleased that weather would put on such a display. "This," I say, "is typical."

And then the rain lets up. Never a hint of hail. Not a single tornado. Just finished. The clouds move on. The glow of sunset emerges and tints the world sepia.

The land-line rings. I race across the shed to snatch it before it goes to the message. It's Maureen. The show will proceed. The band is almost ready to start. They'd like me to sit in on guitar.

She knows how much I love to sit in.

Asa and I drive back to Joes, guitar and amp in the back seat. The dirt road is wet-clay slick. My car prefers sideways to forward. Take it easy, that's all. Twenty minutes later, we're in the upstairs apartment where Glenda is making flower crowns for everybody.

Everybody is: Bert and Joe and Mia and Carolyn and Maureen and Maureen's collaborator, Kirsten. Plus me and Asa and the band.

The band is huddled around a pile of instruments and electronics. They seem to have successfully set up my PA. As a soundman, I would have recommended that they skip that particular hassle, what with the room being only slightly larger than a minivan. However, in fleeing the storm with Asa, and thereby neglecting my sound-guy duties, I'd forfeited my right to offer advice.

On lead vocals tonight is Saphiella. She's maybe twenty-five years old with center-parted straight-hair. She exudes optimism and body positivity. She's humble, very hippie. I dig her.

On bass is Pretty Larry, a thin, bearded middle-aged gentleman outfitted in a leather biker vest. Somewhere on that vest will be a patch advertising the name of his particular affiliation. I do not allow my eyes to seek out that patch, as it's sure to reveal some shit I don't want to know. Anyway, he excretes the same exaggerated friendliness that you see from guns-rights advocates and Jesus-spreaders. If we're going to get along, I have to play along.

The guitarist and boss of the band is a wraith named Bracken. Bracken is somewhere between forty and 1,000 years old. He is undernourished, with crazy eyes and face of ancient leather. He snatches a cable out of Pretty Larry's grip. "Not like that."

Bracken introduces himself by launching into the second paragraph of a conversation we haven't yet started.

"And here," he waves his phone at me, "is our backing band. It's real drums and bass and anything else we need. I've got over 12,000 songs on this thing. You'll fucking love it. No drums to haul around. Better, no drummer. Ha." He notices my amplifier, which is beautiful and handmade. "You a gear guy?"

I say I am not. I just build things. This will be the amp's debut performance. I joke that it might blow up.

Bracken skips ahead a couple more paragraphs. "We usually use an XP345 array. You ever hear of Red Rocks? It's the exact one they use. Too big for this room, obviously. Very handy, though, when you're playing for thousands of people. You sure you can hang with us?"

I assure him that I can hang. I have altogether too much experience following unfamiliar musicians thru the thickets of unfamiliar songs. It might be the only thing I'm truly good at.

. . .

I'm sitting on a barstool, quietly warming up. Mia presses a flower crown on my head. I flinch. She tells me to suck it up. Everyone wears a crown. I do not protest.

Bracken whispers at his telephone, "Work for me, baby." He presses a finger against the screen and his invisible rhythm section starts playing the Melissa Etheridge song about the window. Conversations go quiet. The audience has endured a thunderstorm, an extremely dodgy flight of wet stairs, and roughly two hours of watching Bracken futz with wires and knobs. They're ready for something to happen, and they've been drinking.

Bracken's bandmates are enjoying a smoke on the deck, so Bracken pauses the invisible band, stomps to the porch, and lights a cigarette of his own. Saphiella and Pretty Larry finish their cigarettes before Bracken finishes his. They join me in the living room in front of the humming amps.

The audience conversations have resumed.

Saphiella is arranging a pillow on the floor. "I like to sit when I sing."

As we wait for Bracken to inhale his smoke, Pretty Larry and I play licks at each other. It's a way of sizing one another up. Calibrating expectations. He's competent. My beautiful amplifier is sounding good.

Saphiella breaks into an impromptu version of the Janis Joplin *a capella* charmer about a coveted Mercedes Benz. She's got pipes, this one, and the whole room sings along.

The song winds down. Bracken returns, exhales a lungful of smoke into the room, and says, "Rock and load!"

He presses his phone and the invisible band re-starts the Melissa Etheridge song. Bracken and Pretty Larry join the invisible band and pluck 'n' strum the introduction and then Saphiella sings, "I would dial the numbers just to listen to your breath." She is luminous. This might work out.

I've never played this song. It'll take a verse before I'm up to speed. Bracken's fingers are all kinds of crooked—either from a motorcycle accident or the shingles, I can't remember—so I can't see what chords he's playing. It's okay, I've got ears.

The audience is nodding along, ready for me to unleash my regionally-famous chops. I start with a steel guitar lick.

Kirsten shouts, "Something's burning."

Maureen says, "Your amp is on fire." She's referring to my amp. Technically, it's just smoking. One of the power tubes has red-plated. It's glowing like a poker drawn from a forge. I need to kill the power before the glass melts. I do so without injuring myself. Beautiful new handmade amp blues. My show is over.

Bracken pauses the invisible band. Saphiella offers me the use of her amp, which I had not previously noticed.

I say, "You play guitar?"

Bracken says, "It's for her kazoo." Like, duh.

The invisible band kicks off take three of the Etheridge song. The visible band joins in. Saphiella becomes luminous again. I've got the key and the chords and I make a little fill in response to a lyric. Saphiella's amp is on the other side of the room. I can barely hear what I'm playing.

Bracken pauses the song.

"You gotta turn down, bud."

"?"

Bracken reaches to Saphiella's amp and rotates a knob counter-clockwise. "You're good now."

Take four. Bracken's guitar has gotten loud. So loud, in fact, that the visible band can no longer hear the invisible band. We are playing the same song, but in a bewildering variety of tempi. We sound like pall-bearers limping a coffin across a pile of rubble.

Bracken stops the song. Twiddles a knob. Curses at his phone.

The audience is huddled against the far wall, cradling drinks, adjusting their flower crowns.

Bracken says, "Who's ready for some Sheryl Crow?"

The audience makes a sound that suggests that they're at least open to the idea.

This time, before the visibles can join the invisibles, Maureen raises a hand. "Hang on. I'm sorry, but an elderly woman is trying to sleep downstairs. The bass drum is really loud. Would you be —"

Bracken says, "No it isn't."

"Yes it is." Maureen's a drummer. She knows loud from not-loud. She knows polite from rude. And I know that Bracken is not living up to the vibe he'd projected on the couch the night that Maureen had first heard him and Saphiella perform a spontaneous acoustic set at Glenda's birthday party.

"Whatever." Bracken twiddles. Pokes at his phone. New song. Sheryl Crow has given way to Tom Petty, and we've quickly locked in with our digital bandmates. Luminous Saphiella beseeches us to stop draggin' her heart around. Tell it, Saphiella.

Bracken has decided to shout out the song's chords for my convenience. This is not necessary. First of all, he's shouting the wrong chords. Secondly, I have turned my guitar's volume knob to zero. Thirdly, Bracken's guidance is louder than Saphiella's vocals and this is annoying the audience.

Shouting aside, the song proceeds thru choruses and verses and one inaudible guitar solo. I see mouths singing along. The ending is successful, in that we eventually all stop playing.

The audience applauds with a boisterousness that is entirely out of proportion to the quality of what they've just experienced.

"Sweet!" claims Bracken. "Time for a smoke break. Stick around."

The band heads to the porch, shaking cigarettes out of packs. As soon as they're outside, we hear Bracken lay into Pretty Johnny for missing a note in one of the songs we didn't finish.

. . .

You know what I want? I want to tell somebody, anybody, about my wacky day in Englewood. But everybody's in their own heads right now. Anyway, my day of self-actualization cannot compete with the tragedy unfolding before us.

The band has played one fucking song. My amp is crispy. My guitar is a prop. We're subject to the whims of a man who has mistaken this ad hoc house party for a Super Bowl halftime show.

The gig was supposed to start at six o'clock. It's nearly ten-thirty, folks have driven great distances to be here, and we're all just waiting for one thing to go right.

Maybe one song was enough.

Asa is sitting near me. Thanks to our game of H-O-R-S-E in the extremely loud shed, we are bonded. I can see that he is suffering. He can see that I am suffering. On the deck, the cigarettes in the fingers of the band are growing short. I ask Asa if he wants to split. He is cool with that. I tell Maureen we're splitting. She is envious, but is compelled to stay until she's relatively certain that the band will not set the house on fire.

Asa drives us home on the snot-slick dirt road. I'm pleased that he's notching up yet another Joes experience. We get to the house, sit in the kitchen, talk about dogs.

Headlights shine the window, tires crunch the driveway. Maureen has returned, along with the other four-to-six Denver friends who will be crashing here tonight. In a few moments, they will tumble into the house and enthusiastically recap the day.

To the gentle and kind man who kicked my ass in H-O-R-S-E, I say, "I'm not here."

I sprint to the bedroom, shut the door, and crawl into bed and close my eyes. Chatter filters thru the door.

. . .

I'm still pretending I'm asleep when Maureen enters the room and kisses me goodnight.

patterns of the past

A Brief History of Colcha Embroidery in Colorado

Trent Segura

Colcha embroidery is a Hispanic textile art shaped by Anglo and Indigenous craft traditions, primarily found in Colorado and New Mexico. The term "colcha" is Spanish for bed covering or quilt, but in the American Southwest it refers to the wool embroidery used to adorn blankets during the Spanish settlement. This traditional embroidery employs a specialized stitch called the colcha stitch—a long straight stitch, secured with smaller tacking stitches, and layered to fill out simple designs.

Following the Mexican-American War, the prevalence of colcha embroidery waned in the Southwest as commercially produced textiles and Eastern quilting traditions began to spread westward. However, throughout the 20th century, there were efforts to revive the craft, especially in New Mexico. Key revitalization efforts included the Carson Colcha cottage industry by Frances Varos Graves, Arte Antiguo in the Española Valley, and initiatives by the Spanish Colonial Arts Society and Spanish Market in Santa Fe. In the 1930s, artist Rebecca Salsbury Strand James, originally from New York, learned colcha embroidery in Taos from her neighbor Jesusita Acosta Peralta. James created both traditional and pictorial works, which were showcased in the 1960s at the Museum of International Folk Art in Santa Fe, marking a series of colcha embroidery exhibitions throughout the decade.

In 1972, the Museum of International Folk Art invited Chilean artist Carmen Benavente Orrego-Salas to curate an exhibition featuring embroideries from artists she worked with in Nihue, Chile. These pieces depicted everyday rural life in a pictorial and narrative manner. Carmen was subsequently invited by the museum to conduct workshops across Northern New Mexico, where she shared various techniques she learned from English crewel and creative embroidery books. She encouraged artists to draw inspiration from their daily lives and to create their own designs. In the late 1970s the Denver-based nonprofit The Virginia Neal Blue Center for Colorado Women (VNB) hired Carmen to teach embroidery workshops in Colorado's San Luis Valley.

> That's when we first met Carmen Salas, you know? She gave us a two-weeks training on our embroidering and it was really exciting... Oh she said, "well just do your own drawings. Do your own drawings... the picture is more important if you draw it your own way. It's a true picture because nobody else will be able to draw what you draw. You're not copying or anything, it's just what you see." And she said, "draw your past. Your present. What is really real."
> —Tiva Trujillo (Saguache, CO), Los Testamentos, 1979

The VNB recruited poor rural women from the towns of Del Norte, San Luis, and Saguache to produce embroideries that could be sold, offering women a way to supplement their income. The nonprofit provided materials, instruction, and a small hourly wage —or paid per square inch—in exchange for completed embroideries. Many of the artists cherished the opportunity to stitch and visit with friends, many felt that the nonprofit did not fairly compensate them for their labor. A receipt from an artist in

Saguache shows that she was paid less than $8 ($34.62 today) for an entire embroidery. Artists created very personal artworks that they would never see again. Dissatisfaction with the program fostered a sense of distrust for outside organizations within these communities and many women stopped embroidering all together.

Efforts began in the 1980's to track down where artworks made in Saguache went after they left the community. In 1993, the Saguache Public Library was the site of a homecoming celebration for a beloved quilt composed of 19 panels made by artists who participated in the local stitching group, La Costura de Saguache. Each panel depicted the historic buildings of town with architectural elements rendered in different stitches. Blanche Cowperthwaite, the former executive director of VNB, donated the quilt to the community at the request of Delores Worley. Delores worked persistently to bring it home and still lives in Saguache, turning 95 last April. Today the quilt hangs in the Colorado Room of the Saguache Public library.

In 2018 the grassroots community organization HEART of Saguache initiated the San Luis Valley Colcha Embroidery Project in partnership with The Range, an art space in Downtown Saguache. This project supports exhibitions, workshops, scholarship, and colcha embroidery artists throughout the Valley. Local artists teach in Valley communities and gather frequently to celebrate and exhibit their artworks. Artists Adrienne Garbini and Trent Segura work with artists, family members, scholars, and institutions to research the history of San Luis Valley/Colorado colcha embroidery and locate artworks made in the region. The mystery of where the art went makes it difficult to organize exhibitions, but in 2023, there was a major breakthrough with an exhibition at the Arvada Center for the Arts and Humanities that resulted in the return of nine artworks found in the City of Arvada Collection to artists and surviving family members.

. . .

Today colcha embroidery in Colorado is a beloved artform with many new practitioners drawn to its colorful and complex history. The Colorado tradition of colcha embroidery is a vibrant fusion of stitches, materials, and techniques. Artists explore diverse approaches to creating artwork, often depicting landscapes, architecture, memories, folklore, and storytelling. Their subjects range from portraits and abstract designs to animals, cartoons, and traditional New Mexican motifs. Some artists translate photographs into embroidery, while others freehand their designs or plan their compositions on paper beforehand. Many use commercial wool Colonial Persian 3-ply yarn in a rich spectrum of colors on cotton cloths, while some incorporate hand-produced yarn and sabanilla wool cloths from New Mexico. The artworks exemplify the unique talents and memories of Colorado artists and hold great promise for the continuation of the tradition.

the authors & artists

Teague von Bohlen

...is an Associate Professor of Fiction at the University of Colorado Denver, where he runs the student newspaper *The Sentry* and serves as Fiction Editor for the literary magazine *Copper Nickel*. He works the literary, pop-culture, and social/political commentary beats for the alt-weekly *Westword*, and his short fiction has been seen nationwide. His first novel, *The Pull of the Earth*, won the Colorado Book Award, and he's the co-author of the student-strategy textbook *The Snarktastic Guide to College Success*. His first collection of stories, a flash fiction/photography mash-up called *Flatland*, was named a finalist for the Colorado Book Award in 2020. He's currently shopping a completed ghost-story novel called *The Normal Home*, also set in the Midwest heartland, working on an ultra-nerdy LitRPG book with an old friend, and has started his next literary novel as well, this one set in both Tucson and Denver.

He makes a home in Colorado now, and grew an abiding love for the desert in his time in Arizona. But his corn-fed heart never left Illinois.

Anita Mumm

... is a developmental editor, ghostwriter, and publishing consultant. She grew up miles from a paved road in western Kansas, surrounded by unbroken stretches of wheat, pastureland, and blue sky. Nowadays, her home is in the Rocky Mountains of Colorado.

Claire Boyles

...is a writer, mom, and former farmer who lives and writes in Colorado. A 2022 Whiting Award winner in fiction, she is the author of *Site Fidelity,* which won the 2022 High Plains Book Award for Short Stories. *Site Fidelity* was also longlisted for the PEN/Robert W. Bingham Award and the Reading the West Award and was a finalist for both the Colorado Book Award and the WILLA Literary Award in Multiform Fiction. Her writing has appeared in VQR, Kenyon Review, Boulevard, and Masters Review, among others. She is a Peter Taylor Fellow for the Kenyon Review Writing Workshops and has received support from the Kimmel Harding Nelson Foundation, the Bread Loaf Orion Environmental Writers Workshop, and the Community of Writers. She teaches in Eastern Oregon University's MFA in Creative and Environmental Writing and in Western Colorado University's MFA in Nature Writing .

Erin Harper

...makes films that interpret her rural upbringing in Colorado. As part of that signature, her collaborations have included adapting the writing of Colorado author Gregory Hill.

Her latest short film, *Veral, is* adapted from Hill's short story *Now Museum, Now You Don't—a* springboard to a new original series, *Aje.*

Veral screened at festivals nationwide, including Toronto

Shorts International, AxWound, Shockfest, Maryland Film Feast, NYWIFT Shorts Fest, and Asheville Fringe, and broadcast on NY Public Television for CUNY TV.

As a one-woman band, she makes and self-distributes an ongoing observational short series about farmers across the country and, along this production route, seeks out teaching film in rural settings.

Married to a musician, Erin often works with many musicians, shooting live recording settings, performances, and music videos. She recently shot and edited Maria Schneider's live big band, Grammy-award-winning and Pulitzer Prize Finalist *Data Lords.* Erin's latest project will be directing an international collaboration with Eleanor Dubinsky and local musicians in Luanda, Angola, where she will also teach filmmaking to local youth.

Erin co-directed and edited the feature documentary *My Wild Heart* and was the cinematographer of Barbara Hammer's award-winning films, *Maya Deren's Sink* and Camera on Guggenheim fellowship winner *Welcome to This House*. Erin produced Greenwell's award-winning Sundance Film *My Best Day* in 2012.

Erin received her BS from Northwestern University in Theatre and Dance and an MFA in Writing/Directing and Production at CCNY.

Erin Greenwell

...is a New York Filmmaker who received her BFA from NYU Tisch School of the Arts and her MFA in Writing and Directing from the City College of New York.

Erin directed the feature film *My Best Day*, which premiered at the Sundance Film Festival. She also co-produced and edited *Hunting in Wartime*, a documentary profiling the extraordinary stories of Tlingit Vietnam War veterans that aired on public television stations nationwide.

Erin served as editor on *Yomeddine*, an international feature narrative that was nominated for a Palme d'Or Award at the Cannes Film Festival. It was also submitted by Egypt for consideration of Best International Film for the 91st Oscars.

Erin's recent fiction short, *Skin the Wire*, premiered at the NY Shorts Festival, and her doc/animation hybrid short, *The Phoenix and The Dove*, a remote collaboration with Bedford Hills College Program alumna Connie Leung, is in final post-production.

Teaching awards include the Outstanding Faculty Award for Communication + Media Arts and the C-TIE Award for Innovative Teaching.

Maureen Hearty

...is an artist, gardener, musician, and community organizer who uses art, music, and horticulture as tools for community activation. Maureen currently lives on the high plains in Joes, Colorado; playing music with her husband, building creative community opportunities and transforming metal waste into sculptures. Maureen has spent the last 10 years working on the activation of entropic rural places and generating creative community engagement. She is the co-founder and co-director of Prairie Sea Projects. She in love with Gregory Hill. And her ditch-driving skills are improving.

Nina Elder

...creates projects that reveal humanity's dependence on, and interruption of, the natural world. With a focus on changing cultures and ecologies, Nina advocates for collaboration, fostering relationships between institutions, artists, scientists and diverse communities. She is the co-founder of the Wheelhouse Institute, a women's climate leadership initiative. Nina lectures as a visiting artist/scholar at universities, develops publicly engaged programs, and consults with organizations that seek to grow through interdisciplinary programming.

Nina's artwork is widely exhibited and has been featured in Art in America, VICE Magazine, and on PBS. Her research has been supported by the Andy Warhol Foundation, the Rauschenberg Foundation award for Arts & Activism, the Pollock Krasner Foundation, and the Mellon Foundation. She has recently held positions as an Art + Environment Research Fellow at the Nevada Museum of Art, a Polar Lab Research Fellow at the Anchorage Museum, and a Researcher in Residence in the Art and Ecology Program at the University of New Mexico. She migrates between rural New Mexico and site-specific projects.

Zach Boddicker

...is the author of two novels: *Rise of the Haugenberrys* and *The Essential Carl Mahogany.* He lives out by the airport, and occasionally writes, records, and performs songs with the band 4H Royalty, among others.

Emmett Wilder

...is an author and existentialist exploring themes of death, decay, and redemption in rural America. When he isn't writing, he's likely somewhere in the Colorado foothills picking his six-string or spending time with his loyal canine, Addison Wesley.

Andrea Moore

...is an artist, community organizer, and nonprofit consultant based in the American West. She writes and performs original stories, exploring themes of social and cultural belonging and incorporating installation art and traditional crafts. Andrea also speaks and teaches on the topics of creative activism, community building, inclusion, accessibility, and global citizenry. She is the co-founder and former executive director of The Wayfaring Band, a Denver-based nonprofit that creates adventure travel and immersive learning opportunities for adults with intellectual and developmental disabilities. Learn more about Andrea at AndreaMooreArts.com.

Gregory Hill

...writes fiction, builds flammable amplifiers, does music, yippity yoobers, hooh-hah, ding-a-ling. He oversees Daisy Dog Press, Bing Audio Electronics, and the Sparky the Dog Record Label/Studio/Entertainment Empire. He is in love with Maureen Hearty.

Trent Segura

....is an artist, researcher, and designer based out of Denver, CO. He first learned about colcha embroidery from a family presentation on his late great-aunt Tiva Trujillo in 2001. Tiva was a member of the stitching group, La Costura de Saguache ("The Stitch of Saguache) She produced around 27 artworks before her premature death in 1980. Tiva's iconic map of the San Luis Valley was made in 1978-1979, employing over 17 stitches to depict the Valley and can be viewed on occasion at the History Colorado museum in Denver. Trent was taught by the artist Delores Worley who was a member of La Costura de Saguache with Tiva in the 1970s. He's received instruction from Julia Gomez of Santa Fe and NEA Heritage Fellow, Josie Lobato of San Luis. Trent works at the HEART of Saguache where he collaborates on the The San Luis Valley Colcha Embroidery Project, an effort supports exhibitions, workshops, scholarship, and colcha embroidery artists. He is also a member of M12 STUDIO, a contemporary arts collective based out of Colorado.

Anonymouses

...are the brave souls who attended one or both of the Prairie Futures writing workshops: Judy Hill, Amy Carbone, Terry Welty, Jan Wilkowski, Katie Drullinger, Pat Covert, Terry Covert, Kris VanDeraa, Christi Herrick, Savannah Rothbauer, Aurora Rothbauer, Tonya Rothbauer, Elizabeth Hickman, and Beth Wenstrom.

Kirsten Stoltz

...is a collaborative and interdisciplinary artist and designer who focuses on community-based art projects in rural areas. In 2016, she co-founded Prairie Sea Projects with Maureen Hearty. Born in Yuma, Colorado, Stoltz's family has deep roots in the region. Her paternal grandparents owned and operated the Alma Motel in Joes until the 1980s, and her maternal grandparents founded Shop-All, the only independent grocery store in the area. Stoltz has held curatorial positions at the Boulder Museum of Contemporary Art and the Center for Contemporary Art in Santa Fe. She is also a former member of M12 Studio. In 2019, Stoltz's essay "A Country Social" was published in The Rural, a volume within the Documents of Contemporary Art series. She has also edited several books, including Weather Report: Art and Climate Change by Lucy R. Lippard (2007) and Parallaxis: Fifty-five Points of View (1996).

Hi-Lo
MOTEL
American Owned
FREE WiFi &
Cable
812

www.ingramcontent.com/pod-product-compliance
Ingram Content Group UK Ltd.
Pitfield, Milton Keynes, MK11 3LW, UK
UKHW040022200726
13854UKWH00001B/301

9 798218 488659